THE DECAMERON PROJECT

From the editors of The New York Times Magazine, including Caitlin Roper, Claire Gutierrez, Sheila Glaser, and Jake Silverstein ...

'The stories here range from the oddly familiar – masks, social distancing, empty supermarket shelves – to the brilliantly absurd or the eerily beautiful.

Edwidge Danticat's One Thing is heartbreaking, as a wife plays Nina Simone's Wild Is The Wind to her hospitalised husband over the phone '16 times for the 16 weeks they've been married'.

While Colm Toibin's infectious tale of haphazard domestic bliss, bad dancing and a bike ride is a joyous, hopeful celebration of life'
Daily Mail

'Editors at the New York Time Magazine looked for short stories that would both distract from the current moment and make it more comprehensible. The result is a brilliantly varied assortment of tales'
New Statesman

THE DECAMERON PROJECT ✹

29 NEW STORIES FROM THE PANDEMIC

The New York Times Magazine

Illustrations by Sophy Hollington

SCRIBNER

London   New York   Toronto   Sydney   New Delhi

First published in the United States by Scribner, an imprint of
Simon & Schuster, Inc., 2020
First published in Great Britain by Scribner, an imprint of
Simon & Schuster UK Ltd, 2020
This paperback edition published 2021

Copyright © *The New York Times*, 2020

The right of *The New York Times* to be identified as the author of this work has
been asserted in accordance with the Copyright, Designs and Patents Act, 1988.
SCRIBNER and design are registered trademarks of The Gale Group, Inc., used under
licence by Simon & Schuster Inc.

1 3 5 7 9 10 8 6 4 2

Simon & Schuster UK Ltd
1st Floor
222 Gray's Inn Road
London WC1X 8HB

www.simonandschuster.co.uk
www.simonandschuster.com.au
www.simonandschuster.co.in

Simon & Schuster Australia, Sydney
Simon & Schuster India, New Delhi

A CIP catalogue record for this book is available from the British Library

Paperback ISBN: 978-1-3985-0218-5
eBook ISBN: 978-1-3985-0216-1

Printed in the UK by CPI Group (UK) Ltd, Croydon, CR0 4YY

CONTENTS

Preface by Caitlin Roper   ix

Introduction by Rivka Galchen   xiii

Recognition by Victor LaValle   1

A Blue Sky Like This by Mona Awad   11

The Walk by Kamila Shamsie   23

Tales from the L.A. River by Colm Tóibín   29

Clinical Notes by Liz Moore   41

The Team by Tommy Orange   51

The Rock by Leïla Slimani   59

Impatient Griselda by Margaret Atwood   67

Under the Magnolia by Yiyun Li   77

Outside by Etgar Keret   83

Keepsakes by Andrew O'Hagan   89

The Girl with the Big Red Suitcase
    by Rachel Kushner   99

The Morningside by Téa Obreht   113

Screen Time by Alejandro Zambra   123

How We Used to Play by Dinaw Mengestu   135

Line 19 Woodstock/Glisan by Karen Russell   143

If Wishes Was Horses by David Mitchell   159

Systems by Charles Yu   171

The Perfect Travel Buddy by Paolo Giordano   183

An Obliging Robber by Mia Couto   195

Sleep by Uzodinma Iweala   201

The Cellar by Dina Nayeri   213

That Time at My Brother's Wedding
    by Laila Lalami   225

A Time of Death, the Death of Time
    by Julián Fuks   231

Prudent Girls by Rivers Solomon   239

Origin Story by Matthew Baker   251

To the Wall by Esi Edugyan   261

Barcelona: Open City by John Wray   269

One Thing by Edwidge Danticat   281

Acknowledgments   291

Contributors   293

PREFACE BY
CAITLIN ROPER

n March 2020, bookstores began selling out of a book from the 14th century—Giovanni Boccaccio's *The Decameron*, a collection of nested tales told by and for a group of women and men sheltering in place outside of Florence as the plague ravages the city. In the United States, we were beginning to self-isolate, learning what it meant to quarantine, and many readers were looking for guidance from this ancient book. As the coronavirus began its spread across the world, the novelist Rivka Galchen approached *The New York Times Magazine* and told us that she'd like to write a story recommending Boccaccio's *Decameron* to help readers understand the present moment. We loved the idea, but wondered, instead, what if we made our own *Decameron*, filled with new fiction written during quarantine?

We began reaching out to writers with a request for pitches—some sense of the stories they hoped to tell. A few were working on novels and didn't have time. One was taking care of small children and hadn't figured out how, and if, he could write under the circumstances. Another wrote: "I'm afraid the fiction-writing part of my brain is not finding any inspiration from the current crisis." We understood. We weren't sure if our idea had legs.

But then, as the virus gripped New York City, and we were scared, and grieving, we began hearing something else, something hopeful—interest, and tantalizing story ideas. Novelist John Wray said he wanted to write "about a young man in Spain who rents his dogs to people in order to help them duck curfew restrictions by pretending to be walking their pets." Mona Awad's idea began: "On her 40th birthday, a woman visits an exclusive spa in order to get one of their infamous facials as a special gift to herself. When she's there, they offer her a highly experimental treatment that involves the removal of certain bad memories in order to truly brighten, plump, and smooth the skin. . . ." Charles Yu told us he had a few ideas, "but the one that excites me the most is a story told from two points of view: the virus and the Google search algorithm." Margaret Atwood's pitch for the story she would like to write was: "It is told to a group of quarantined Earthlings by an alien from a distant planet who has been sent to Earth as part of an interstellar aid package." That's it, that was the whole pitch. How could we say no? We wanted to read all of these stories. In fact, we assigned too many to fit in a magazine issue. We quickly realized, with pain, that we had to stop reaching out to writers.

When the stories began rolling in, even as we were plunged deeper into one of the scariest experiences of our lives, we knew these writers were creating art. We hadn't expected the degree to which they would be able to turn the horror of our current moment into something so powerful. It was a reminder that the best fiction can both transport you far from yourself but also, somehow, help you understand exactly where you are.

The magazine issue was published on July 12, as the virus was surging again in the United States. The response from readers was swift and enthusiastic. Our inboxes filled with letters to the editor remarking on the solace provided by these tales. We can think of no greater aspiration for this project, both in its original form and now as the book you hold in your hands, than to provide delight and consolation during a dark and unsteady time. We hope you read it in good health.

LIFESAVING
TALES AN INTRODUCTION BY RIVKA GALCHEN

en young people decide to quarantine outside Florence. It's 1348, in the time of the bubonic plague. The afflicted develop lumps in their groins or armpits, then dark spots on their limbs. Some appear healthy at breakfast but by dinner are sharing a meal, it is said, with their ancestors in another world. Wild pigs sniff and tear at the rags of corpses, then convulse and die themselves. What do these young people do, after fleeing unspeakable suffering and horror? They eat, sing songs, and take turns telling one another stories. In one story, a nun mistakenly wears her own lover's trousers on her head, as a wimple. In another, a heartbroken woman grows basil in a pot that contains her lover's severed head. Most of the stories are silly, some are sad, and none are focused on the plague. This is the structure of Giovanni Boccaccio's *The Decameron*, a book that has been celebrated now for nearly 700 years.

Boccaccio, himself from Florence, most likely began writing *The Decameron* in 1349, the same year his father died, probably of the plague. He finished the book within a few years. It was first read and loved by the very people who watched roughly half their fellow citizens die. The stories in the book are largely not new but are instead reincarnations of old familiar tales. Boccaccio ends *The Decameron* with a joke about how some readers might dismiss him as a lightweight, although, he explains, he weighs a lot. What to make of all his playfulness at such a moment?

Along with many others, in mid-March I watched two rockhopper penguins waddling free at Chicago's Shedd Aquarium. Wellington the penguin took a shine to the belugas. Though at that time I had probably already read dozens of articles about the novel coronavirus, it was those curious, isolated penguins that made the pandemic real for me emotionally, even as the videos also made me smile and were a relief from "the news." In May, three Humboldt penguins visited the uncannily empty halls of the Nelson-Atkins Museum of Art in Kansas City and lingered at the Caravaggio paintings. Those penguins themselves had something of the startle of art—the reveal of the ever-present real that's hidden, paradoxically, by information.

Reality is easy to miss, maybe because we're looking at it all the time. My daughter, who is six, had little to say and few questions to ask about the pandemic, save for now and again floating a plan: to tear the coronavirus into a million pieces and bury it in the ground. She found it too upsetting a "story" to think about it directly. But when the news was about personal protective equipment, her figurines began to wear armor made out of foil chocolate wrappers, string, and tape. Later they were wrapped in cotton balls. They engaged in detailed battles I didn't understand. In quieter reading moments, my daughter became obsessed with the series Wings of Fire, in which young dragons work to fulfill a prophecy that they will bring an end to war.

When there's a radical and true and important story happening at every moment, why turn to imagined tales? "Art is what makes life more interesting than art," the French Fluxus artist Robert Filliou noted in one of his works, suggesting that we don't catch sight of life at first glance. As if life were one of those trick images, like the skull in the Hans Holbein the Younger painting *The Ambassadors*, which is noticed only when the viewer stands off to the side—looked at straight on, it might be mistaken for driftwood, or not noticed at all. In the Italian of Boccaccio, the word *novelle* means both news and stories. The tales of *The Decameron* are the news in a form the listeners can follow. (The rule of the young people's quarantine was: No news of Florence!) The first story is a comic account of how to deal with a soon-to-be corpse; the comedy gives cover to the catastrophe too familiar to be understood.

But over the course of *The Decameron*, the tone and content of the stories the young people tell one another shifts. The first few days are mostly jokes and irreverence. Then the fourth day is 10 stories in a row on the theme of tragic love. The fifth: stories of lovers who, after terrible accidents or misfortunes, find happiness. Boccaccio writes that during the Black Death the people of Florence stopped mourning or weeping over the dead. After some days away, the young storytellers of his tale are finally able to cry, nominally over imaginary tales of tragic love, but more likely from their own hearts.

The paradox of Boccaccio's escapist stories is that they ultimately return the characters, and readers, to what they have fled. The early stories are set across time and space, while the later stories are often set in Tuscany, or even in Florence specifically. The characters within the stories are in more contemporary and recognizable binds. A corrupt Florentine judge is pantsed by pranksters—everyone laughs. A simpleton called Calandrino is tricked and wronged again and again—should we laugh? By the 10th day, we hear tales of those who behave with nearly unimaginable nobility in the face of a manifestly cruel and unjust world. Under emotional cover—it's only a story—the characters experience hope.

Boccaccio's series of stories told within a frame was itself an old structure made new again. In *One Thousand and One Nights*, the frame is Scheherazade telling stories to her husband, the king. If the king gets bored, he'll kill Scheherazade, as he did his wives before her. The nested stories of the *Panchatantra* show characters—often animals, sometimes people—navigating difficulties, dilemmas, and war. In all these cases, the stories, in one way or another, are lifesaving, even as their being entertaining is one of the main ways they can save a life. Reading stories in difficult times is a way to understand those times, and also a way to persevere through them.

The young people of *The Decameron* didn't leave their city forever. After two weeks away, they decided to return. They returned not because the plague was over—they had no reason to believe it was. They returned because having laughed and cried and imagined new rules for living altogether, they were then able to finally see the present, and think of the future. The novelle of their days away made the novelle of their world, at least briefly, vivid again. *Memento mori*—remember that you must die—is a worthy and necessary message for ordinary times when you might forget. *Memento vivere*—remember that you must live— is the message of *The Decameron*.

RECOGNITION
BY VICTOR LAVALLE

ot easy to find a good apartment in New York City, so imagine finding a good building. No, this isn't a story about me buying a building. I'm talking about the people, of course. I found a good apartment, and a great building, in Washington Heights. Six-story tenement on the corner of 180th and Fort Washington Avenue; a one-bedroom apartment, which was plenty for me. Moved in December 2019. You might already see where this is going. The virus hit, and within four months half the building had emptied out. Some of my neighbors fled to second homes or to stay with their parents outside the city; others, the older ones, the poorer ones, disappeared into the hospital 12 blocks away. I'd moved into a crowded building and suddenly I lived in an empty house.

And then I met Pilar.

"Do you believe in past lives?"

We were in the lobby, waiting for the elevator. This was right after the lockdown started. She asked, but I didn't say anything. Which isn't the same as saying I didn't respond. I gave my tight little smile while looking down at my feet. I'm not rude, just fantastically shy. That condition doesn't go away, not even during a pandemic. I'm a Black woman, and people act surprised when they discover some of us can be awkward, too.

"There's no one else here," Pilar continued. "So I must be talking to you."

Her tone managed to be both direct and, somehow, still playful. As the elevator arrived, I looked toward her, and that's when I saw her shoes. Black-and-white pointed oxfords; the white portion had been painted to look like piano keys. Despite the lockdown, Pilar had taken the trouble to slip on a pair of shoes that nice. I was returning from the supermarket wearing my raggedy old slides.

I pulled the elevator door open and finally looked at her face.

"There she is," Pilar said, the way you might compliment a shy bird for settling on your finger.

Pilar might've been 20 years older than me. I turned 40 the same month I moved into the building. My mom and dad called to sing "Happy Birthday" from Pittsburgh. Despite the news, they didn't ask me to come home. And I didn't make the request. When we're together, they ask questions about my life, my plans, that turn me into a grouchy teenager again. My father ordered me a bunch of basics, though; he had them shipped. It's how he has always loved me—by making sure I'm well supplied.

"I tried to get toilet paper," Pilar said in the elevator. "But these people are panicking, so I couldn't find any. They think a clean butt is going to save them from the virus?"

Pilar watched me; the elevator reached the fourth floor. She stepped out and held the door open.

"You don't laugh at my jokes, and you won't even tell me your name?"

Now I smiled because it had turned into a game.

"A challenge, then," she said. "I will see you again." She pointed down the hall. "I am in number forty-one."

She let the elevator door go, and I rode up to the sixth floor, unpacked the things I'd bought. At that time I still thought it would all be over soon. It's laughable now. I went into the bathroom. One of the things my dad sent me was 32 rolls of toilet paper. I slipped back down to the fourth floor and left three rolls in front of Pilar's door.

A month later, I was used to logging in to my "remote office," the grid of screens—all our little heads—looked like the open office we once worked in; I probably spoke with my co-workers about as much now as I did then. When the doorbell rang, I leapt at the chance to get away from my laptop. Maybe it's Pilar. I slipped on a pair of buckled loafers; they were raggedy, too, but better than the slippers I wore the last time she saw me.

But it wasn't her.

It was the super, Andrés. Nearly 60, born in Puerto Rico, he had a tattoo of a leopard crawling up his neck.

"Still here," he said, sounding pleasant behind his blue mask.

"Nowhere else to go."

He nodded and snorted, a mix between a laugh and a

5

cough. "The city says I got to check every apartment now. Every day."

He carried a bag that rattled like a sack of metal snakes. When I looked, he pulled it open: silver spray-paint cans. "I don't get a answer, and I got to use this."

Andrés stepped to the side. Down the hall; apartment 66. The green door had been defaced with a giant silver "V." So fresh, the letter still dripped.

"'V.' For 'virus'?"

Andrés's eyebrows rose and fell.

"Vacant," he said.

"That's a nicer way to put it, I guess." We stood quietly, him in the hall and me in the apartment. I realized I hadn't put on my mask when I answered, and I covered my mouth when I spoke.

"The city is making you do this?" I asked.

"In some neighborhoods," Andrés said. "Bronx, Queens, Harlem. And us. Hot spots." He took out one of the cans and shook it. The ball bearing clicked and clacked inside. "I'll knock tomorrow," he said. "If you don't answer, I got the keys."

I watched him go.

"How many people are left?" I called out. "In the building?"

He'd already reached the stairs, started down. If he answered, I didn't hear it. I walked onto the landing. There were six apartments on my floor. Five doors had been decorated with the letter "V." No one here but me.

You'd think I would run right down to Pilar's place, but I couldn't afford to lose my job. The landlord hadn't said a word about rent forgiveness. I went back to the computer until end-of-day. I felt such relief when No. 41 hadn't been painted. I knocked until Pilar opened. She wore her mask, just like me now, but I could tell she was smiling. She looked from my face to my feet.

"Those shoes have seen better days," she said, and laughed so joyfully that I hardly even felt embarrassed.

Pilar and I made trips to the supermarket together; two trips to the store each week. We walked side by side, arm's length apart, and when we crossed paths with others, we marched single file. Pilar talked the whole time, whether I was next to her or behind her. I know some people criticize chatty folks, but her chatter fell upon me like a nourishing rain.

She came to New York from Colombia, with a short stay in Key West, Florida, in between. She'd lived in Manhattan, from the bottom to the top, over the span of 40 years. She played piano and idolized Peruchín; had performed with Chucho Valdés. And now she gave lessons to children in her apartment for $35 an hour. Or at least she had done that, until the virus made it unsafe to have them over. I miss them, she said, every time we talked, as four weeks became six, and six became 12. She wondered if she'd ever see her students and their parents again.

I offered to help set up remote piano lessons. I'd use my job's account to set up free chat sessions for her. But this was three months in and Pilar had lost her playful ways. She said: "The screens give the illusion that we're all still connected. But it's not true. The ones who could leave, left. The rest of us? We were abandoned."

She stepped off the elevator.

"Why pretend?"

She scared me. I can see that now. But I told myself I'd become busier. As if I'd transformed. But I fled from her. We were all living on the ledge of despair, so when she said it—"We were abandoned. Why pretend?"—it was as if she spoke from down in that pit. A place I found myself slipping into often enough already. So I went to the store by myself, and I held my breath when the elevator passed the fourth floor.

Meanwhile, Andrés continued to work. I didn't see him. He knocked on the door each morning, and I knocked from the other side. But I saw evidence of his work. Three apartments on the first floor marked with a "V" one week. Next time I went to the store the other three were painted.

Four on the second floor.

Five on the third.

One afternoon I heard him kicking at a door on the fourth floor. Shouting a name I hardly recognized through the muzzle that was his mask. I left my place and walked down. Andrés looked shrunken at the door of No. 41. He kicked at it desperately.

"Pilar!" he shouted again.

He turned with surprise when I appeared. His eyes were red. The fingers of his right hand were entirely silver now; it looked permanent. I wondered if he'd ever be able to wash off the spray paint. But how could he, if the job was never done?

"I left my keys," he said. "I gotta get them."

"I'll stay," I said.

He sprinted down the stairs. I stood by the door, didn't bother knocking. If that kicking didn't wake her, what could I do?

"Is he gone?"

I almost collapsed.

"Pilar! Were you messing with him?"

"No," she said through the door. "But I wasn't waiting on him. I was waiting around for you."

I sat so my head was at about the same level as her voice. I heard her labored breathing through the door. "It's been a while," she finally said.

I rested the side of my head against the cool door. "I'm sorry."

She sniffed. "Even women like us are scared of women like us."

I lowered my mask, as if it were getting in the way of what I truly needed to say. But I still couldn't find the words.

"Do you believe in past lives?" she said.

"That's the first thing you ever asked me."

"When I saw you by the elevator, I knew we'd met before. Recognition. Like seeing a member of my family."

The elevator arrived. Andrés stepped out. I raised my mask and got to my feet. He unlocked the door.

"Be careful," I said. "She's right there."

But when he pushed the door open, the hall sat empty.

Andrés found her in bed. Dead. He came out carrying a bag, my name written on it. Her black-and-white oxfords were inside. A note in the left shoe. Give them back when you see me again.

I have to slip on an extra pair of socks to make them fit, but I wear them everywhere I go.

A BLUE SKY LIKE THIS
BY MONA AWAD

nd now it's your birthday on top of everything else. You've been dreading it. That's what you've been texting friends for days now: I'm dreading it. Adding a pained emoji face. Xs for eyes, open mouth like an O. Making fun of yourself and your silly dread. But the dread is real. That's why you're here in spite of everything. A place you found on the dark web. Open despite the lockdown. A penthouse suite downtown. The dark womb of a treatment room heavy with steam and eucalyptus. The light is so dim and kind. You're lying naked on a heated table. A woman is kneading your face with some sort of goat placenta. You can feel her knuckles digging deeply into your cheek, draining you of lymphatic fluid. Lots of draining to be done, she says softly. "I'm sure," you whisper. "Drain away."

The woman looked ageless in her black suit, her hair pulled back in a tight bun.

Three deep breaths, there you go, she said. I'll take them with you. Shall I take them with you?

She rubbed her hands with essential oil and held them suspended over your nose and mouth. Don't worry, she said,

13

perhaps sensing your fear, your hesitation. We take every precaution. Well, all right. You breathed deeply together. You felt your chests rise and fall.

There, she said. That's better, isn't it?

You heard a water fountain in the distance. Soft music composed of no instruments you recognized. Like the endless gong of some terrible bell. But beautiful.

Now she says: "I'm just going to turn on the light so I can assess your skin. It's a bright light, so I'll be covering your eyes." She presses a damp cotton pad over each of your closed eyelids. You think of pennies on the eyes of the dead. The light's so bright you can feel it through the cotton. Flaming red. Hot on your face. And the fact of her eyes. Looking at you.

"Well," you say at last, because you can't take any more of her silence. "What's the verdict?"

"You've had a difficult year, haven't you?"

You picture yourself alone and afraid in your apartment. Shivering on your island of couch. Body on fire. Breathing as if you were drowning as the tears gushed from your eyes.

"Haven't we all?" you say quietly.

She's silent. The eucalyptus scent is becoming oppressive.

"It's all here, I'm afraid," she says at last. Her finger pads trace your forehead furrows, the deep creases between your brows. The veins around your nose, the folds around your mouth. Nasolabial folds, you found out they were called. Laugh lines that weren't even born from laughing. She

14

touches it all so tenderly that a tear leaks from your eyes. She lifts the cotton pads from your lids and holds a mirror over your face.

"Memory and skin go hand in hand," she says. "Good memories, good skin. Unhappy memories—" And here she trails off. Because the mirror speaks for itself, doesn't it?

"How about we do something about it?" she says in a voice like a caress.

And you say, "What?"

And she says, "First, I have to ask you: How attached are you to your memories?"

You look into the mirror. Your life's miseries imprinted there on your skin. Your pores gaping open at you like silently screaming mouths. The toll of the past year alone casts a grayness that might never be lifted.

And you say to your own reflection: "Not attached. Not attached at all."

Now here you are in the bright light of the late summer afternoon. The sun's still high in the sky, so lovely and golden. There's a bounce to your step as you skip out of the building. You're skipping; why not? It's your birthday after all, isn't it? Haven't forgotten that. You wonder what you have forgotten. You think of the woman rubbing those sleek black discs all over your face—those discs attached to electric cables, hooked up to a machine with dials. The woman turned the dials up like volume knobs, and you tasted metal deep in your teeth. It's funny now to think about how you screamed when you felt electricity crackle along your cranium.

The shop in the building's lobby is closed. More than closed; the front window is shattered as if someone had hurled a brick at the glass. Inside, a bald white mannequin stands naked. A glittering swan purse dangles from her wrist as if she's about to go to a party wearing nothing at all. She stares at you with shining eyes. Red lips in a slight smile. A darkness fills your gut. Dread spreads through your limbs. But then you see yourself reflected in the shattered glass. Glowing. Lifted. Eradicated. That's the word that comes most strongly to mind: "eradicated." Which is odd. Doesn't "eradicate" mean destroy? Your face looks the opposite of destroyed. So what if you're wearing a sad black sack? Your face has all the lightness and life and color you need. To add more color would be almost too much. A slap in someone else's face.

In the taxi home, you smile at yourself in the window, in the rearview mirror, at the cabby, though he doesn't smile back.

"Busy day today?" you ask.

"No," he says, as if you're insane. Is he glaring at you? He's wearing a scarf tied over his mouth and nose so it's hard to tell. Maybe he's sick? With what, you wonder. You wish him well, the poor man. You try to communicate this goodwill with your face. He just stares at you coldly in the mirror until you look away, out the window. The city looks surprisingly empty and dirty. In your lap, your phone buzzes. A text from someone called the Lord of Darkness.

Fine, he says, I'll meet you.

It's your b-day, after all.

Park at six. Bench by the swans.

You scroll up to see earlier texts. I need to see you, you apparently texted the Lord of Darkness only two hours ago. Please. Three times you pleaded. Interesting.

Well, can he really be so terrible if you wanted to see him? Needed to, no less? And he knows you well enough to know that it's your birthday, so . . .

Why don't we meet at a wine bar? you text back.

Wine bar?! he says. Yeah, right. See you at the park.

A date with the Lord of Darkness. It's frightening but also thrilling, isn't it? You look at your face in the partition. You instantly feel calm at the sight of yourself. You picture a sun shining out from behind a mass of gray clouds. You're standing in that wonderful light of the mind, and it's beautiful and it's blinding.

At the park, you try to hand the cabbie cash, but he shakes his head violently. He doesn't want your fucking cash. Pay by card only, please. As you stand there watching him screech down the empty street, you notice the sidewalks are empty. In the park, the grass seems to have grown shaggier, wilder, since the last time you were here. There's one couple walking quickly along the path by the pond, their heads bent low.

You see a man in a black hoodie sitting alone on a park

bench by the swans. The Lord of Darkness, has to be. Sure, you're afraid. Mostly excited. An adventure! You're so up for that right now. As you skip along the gravel path, you pass the couple. You feel relief at the sight of them up close— people! But as you approach, smiling, about to say, Hello! Quiet today, isn't it? Well, at least we have the park all to ourselves, hahahaha! they drift off the path onto the shaggy grass; they walk all the way around a weeping willow to avoid you. And while they do this, they glare at you. You're about to say, What the fuck? when you hear your name.

You look over. It's Ben, your ex-husband. Sitting there on the very edge of the bench, staring at you with sad eyes. He's got a flask in his hand. He looks terrible. Puffy and gaunt at the same time.

"Ben?" you say. "Is that really you?" Of course it's him. You just can't believe the Lord of Darkness is Ben. Probably a little joke you were playing to amuse yourself one night. You got drunk and came up with silly names for your contacts. Too funny. When was the last time you saw him? You try to search your mind, but there's nothing. A stone wall.

"Julia," he says. "It's good to see you."

But he doesn't look like it's good. He's looking at you and frowning. Which is weird, considering how amazing you look. You couldn't have picked a better day to meet your ex, frankly.

"It's good to see you too," you tell Ben. He doesn't smile.

"I picked this bench because it was the longest," he says. "So we could sit on either end." He gestures along the length of the bench. You see that he has placed a bottle of screw-top wine and a small white box on the opposite end. "For your birthday," he says. "Happy birthday."

"Thanks," you say, and immediately remember how weird Ben was. Still is, apparently.

"Don't worry," he says. "I wiped the bottle down. The bench too." He smiles, warily. You notice a face mask dangling from his neck. It's made of a floral-patterned fabric. It looks as if he made it himself with a sewing machine and fabric ripped from a tablecloth. Possibly your old tablecloth.

Looking at the mask sparks something—a coldness—but then it's gone. So his germophobia is getting worse. People get weirder as they get older. Sad, really. It makes you feel tenderness toward him.

You join Ben on the bench. Sip the wine and open the white box. There's a Hostess cupcake inside, which he assures you no one has touched. Great, you say. You smile and wait for him to be devastated by you. But he just keeps looking around as if he's afraid.

"Look, I really can't stay long," he says.

"That's fine." It is fine, you realize. Completely. It's a little empowering to realize this. You take a bite of the cupcake. Ben visibly relaxes. So much so that you feel as if you just agreed to something awful.

You smile at Ben. "What's this about?"

He looks at you, dead serious. "You invited me, remember?"

I need to see you. Please.

19

"Oh, yes. Well. I thought it might be nice to catch up."
Sure. That sounds like you.

Ben looks at you as if you're nuts. He sighs heavily. "Look, Julia, you know I care for you."

"I care for you too, Ben." It's nice to say it back. It feels true.

"But there have to be boundaries," he adds quickly. He looks at you meaningfully from the other side of the bench.

"Absolutely," you agree. "Boundaries are great." What the fuck is he talking about?

"I'm in a relationship, you know that."

He needs a haircut, you notice now. His hair is shaggy and long like the grass.

"Sure." You nod. "Congratulations."

He looks appalled. "Is that all you're going to say?"

His eyes suddenly strike you as strange. Didn't they used to be blue? Now they're just this watery gray, the whites full of red veins.

"What do you want me to say?"

"Look, Julia, that was fucked up the other night, OK? I fucked up, too, I'll admit it. But when you call me up crying like that, what am I supposed to do? I mean, what choice did I have?"

You search your memory for the other night. No night to be found anywhere. You try to picture yourself calling Ben. Tears pouring out of your eyes as you dialed. Just blue sky all around, the most pleasant shade.

"I just came to bring you groceries," he says. "I told you

I was just coming to bring groceries. I would do that for any friend who was sick."

He says the word like a slap. "Sick"? That word seems so wrong for you, for how you feel right now. In spite of Ben. Look at him trying to get under your skin like this. He's the one who's sick. He looks about a thousand years old.

"I was just going to leave them outside the door and walk away," Ben says sadly. "But then that sound." Now he closes his eyes. He looks so pained it's ridiculous.

"What sound?" You think of that terrible, beautiful bell in the treatment room. Its endless gong filling your head even now.

"You," Ben says. "Crying. Sobbing. Gasping through the door. All alone. Begging and begging me to come in."

You watch him shake his head. "It still haunts me, if I'm honest," Ben says, looking at you. Waiting, it seems, for you to be devastated. By the shame of your apparent desperation on this night. This night where your grief made a sound he will never forget and apparently couldn't resist. And that's when you know you and Ben must have fucked. Definitely you fucked the Lord of Darkness. Perhaps this is why he's the Lord of Darkness.

"We were reckless," Ben cries. "I was reckless."

And his voice is like a brick. Trying to shatter you as if you're so breakable. Maybe you were once. You observe this as though you are observing a sad fact from very, very far away. But you can't be shattered now. Even with that cold creeping in, you have the red lips of the mannequin—you feel them curved right now in her slight smile. You look at Ben with shining eyes. Ben turns away to stare at the swans.

"Probably just hay fever, thank God," he says. "You always get it at this time of year, and you always forget and think it's something more sinister. You always think you're dying, Julia. Even before. Even before all this." And here he waves a hand around at the world. The swans, the sky, the weeping trees and the shaggy park, a group of people walking by, all masked, you notice now, homemade masks like Ben or scarves like the cabbie. They stop in their tracks and turn toward you. Glaring at your bare, glowing face. Because whatever all this is, you've forgotten it. It's been eradicated. Lifted away by the woman in the black suit.

Suddenly you want to take Ben's hand and press it to your face. His hand was callused in places, soft in others, and it was always warm and dry as it held yours. You remember that now. You reach your hand across the long expanse of bench. Ben's face darkens. He looks at your hand as if it's a snake before mumbling that he has to go. You wave goodbye to him as he gets up and then you wave hello at the staring people because you might as well, you're already waving. They gape at you in horror. Which is just so tragic. What is there to be afraid of on a day like this? Under a blue sky like this? Such a beautiful day. Your birthday.

THE → WALK
BY KAMILA SHAMSIE

zra swung open the gate and stepped onto the road. Are you sure? her mother said from the garden, where she was walking in circles, one circle every 45 seconds.

Everyone's doing it, even women on their own, Azra said, but she left the gate open as she stood outside, clutching her handbag, which was empty except for the mobile phone that made her feel simultaneously safer and more of a target. Five minutes! Zohra called out, walking toward Azra at her usual brisk pace. Her voice could doubtless be heard halfway down the street. It took me five minutes to walk to you. Less.

That seemed unlikely, given that it took nearly that long to drive between their two houses, but Zohra insisted it was true: the traffic, the one-way streets. Azra closed the gate and heard her mother break away from her loops in the garden to step into the driveway and bolt the gate from inside. Wash your hands, Azra said through the narrow opening between the gate and the wall, and her mother said yes, yes, all right, Ms. Paranoid.

They set off, Zohra a pace ahead and a few feet to the

25

side. There were no sidewalks, so they were walking on the road, but even in ordinary times there was little traffic on this residential street. A few houses down, a woman standing on a balcony raised a hand to the pair. The woman had lived there since the house was built, nearly 25 years ago, just after Azra returned home from university. Azra raised a hand back. First interaction.

Early April and already winter was a memory in Karachi. Azra tugged at her kameez, which was sticking to her skin with the humidity. Zohra had dressed as she would for their regular walks in the park—yoga pants and T-shirt. It had been over three weeks since they last walked in the park, though Zohra still drove there daily to feed the park cats; the security guard, who shared her affection for the animals, unlocked the gates for her.

There was only one topic of conversation, but many different subsets of it. They meandered between the quotidian and the apocalyptic, walking along the straight, eerily silent expanse of a main avenue, until the scent of the sea rendered them silent. It shimmered ahead of them for a while and then they were upon it, the sand stretching out, camel brown, pristine, and the water dove gray beyond it. The food vendors, the dune buggies, the kite-sellers, the couples sitting together on the sea wall, the carloads of families seeking the one place where Karachi's urban snarl turned into a smile: all missing. Two policemen, masked, on horseback, rode up to them.

The policemen directed them to leave. They took a

different route home, zigzagging through narrower, tree-lined streets, stopping to discuss the architecture of houses they'd never thought to notice before, even though they'd lived almost all their lives in these few square miles of their megacity. Quite by accident, they found themselves on a road that was filled with walkers, several of whom they knew. Everyone waved, everyone was delighted to see one another and made a great show of keeping a distance, even when they weren't. Preadolescents zipped past on bicycles, unaccompanied by adults. It was the closest thing to a street party this neighborhood had ever known. Azra shouted a greeting to an old school friend, unconcerned by the pitch of her voice, the attention she might draw to herself. Her handbag swung loosely by her side, unclutched. In that moment, the world felt like a better place than it had ever been—generous, safe.

When this is all over, maybe we can sometimes walk here instead of endlessly round the track in the park, Zohra said. Maybe, Azra said.

TALES FROM THE L.A. RIVER
BY. COLM TÓIBÍN

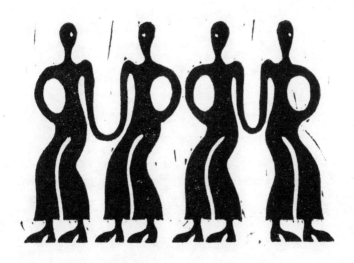

kept a diary during the lockdown. I began by writing the date of my own personal shutdown—March 11, 2020—and the place, Highland Park, Los Angeles. On the first day, I copied down a sign on a camper van I saw that morning: "Smile. You Are Being Filmed."

After that first entry, I could think of nothing else. Nothing much happened after that.

I wish I could say that I was up each morning writing a new chapter, but I lazed in bed. Later, as the day wore on, I grew busy deploring my boyfriend's taste in music, made more appalling by the new speakers H. had bought that blared out clearly what had once blared out vaguely.

Mankind is divided into those who started to listen to Bach and Beethoven in their late teens and those who did not. H. did not; instead he had a huge collection of vinyl, hardly any of which was classical, and not much of which I liked.

And H. and I had not read any of the same books. His first language was French, and his mind was speculative.

31

Thus, in one room he was busy with Jacques and Gilles while in another I was reading Jane and Emily.

He read Harry Dodge; I read David Lodge.

There was a writer who lived in a small midwestern city. I had devoured his two books and liked how emotionally exposed he became in his fiction. Even though I had never met him, I did really want him to be happy. I was delighted to read online that this writer had a boyfriend and to see some posts from him about the happy domestic life they were living. H. had actually met him, and he, too, was pleased that the writer had settled down with someone he loved.

Soon, we began to check out the writer's posts. His boyfriend had flowers waiting for him when he returned to their house. We looked at a photo of the flowers.

And the novelist made cookies, or so his post told us, and he and his boyfriend watched films every night that were a revelation to them both.

For all of us, there are shadow people, shadow places, shadow episodes. Sometimes they take up more space than the paleness of what actually happens.

That paleness makes me shiver, but the shadows make me wonder.

I loved thinking about the shadow novelist and his boyfriend.

And I tried to imagine a narrative of domestic bliss,

sharing space and music and novels and movies, posting online about our love.

But no matter how I dreamed, we could not actually agree at night about which movie to watch. When we decided, Week 1, to look at films set in Los Angeles, they included *Mulholland Drive* and *Body Double*, the first too slow-moving for me and the second too rhetorically ominous. H. not only loved both movies but, because he knew about film, wished to have a discussion about how images from one film could bleed into another, how many hidden references and secret gestures a film contained.

I had only ever gone to the cinema to amuse myself. The hour before bedtime became tense as H. followed me around the house with news of what these films really meant.

That was when I loved him most: He was so earnest and excited by film, by the ideas and images generated on the screen, so eager to keep the conversation at a serious level.

But on the bad nights, I could not help myself. I could only respond: "That film is rubbish! It is an insult to my intelligence!" in response to his detailed and pertinent quotes from Godard and Godot and Guy Debord.

I went through the names of the great gay couples from history—Benjamin Britten and Peter Pears, Gertrude Stein and Alice B. Toklas, Christopher Isherwood and Don Bachardy. Why were they always cooking together, or making drawings of each other, or one writing songs for the other to sing?

Why were we the only ones like us?

It might have been a good time for me and H. to behave like adults for a change and finally and joyfully begin to read each other's favorite books.

Instead we read more of our own favorite books. When it came to culture, he was Jack Sprat, who could eat no fat, and I was his wife, who could eat no lean.

What I enjoy most is when something that I take seriously is laughed at by someone else, or when something I think ludicrous is taken seriously by all others.

When the lockdown began, I thought the L.A. River and all its tributaries were comic. Soon I would learn the truth. And when the whole social distancing was all halfway over, I hoped never to hear another note, if note was the word, of a song called "Little Raver," by Superpitcher, much favored by H. and played loudly by him.

I cannot drive and cannot cook. I cannot dance. I cannot scan a page or send a photo by email. I have never willingly used a vacuum cleaner or knowingly made a bed.

It is hard to justify all of this to someone in whose house you live. I hinted that all my failures came from a maimed childhood, and when that did not work, I suggested, without having any evidence, that untidiness belonged to deep thinkers, people willing to change the world. Marx was untidy; Henry James was a slob; there is no evidence that James Joyce ever cleaned up after himself; Rosa Luxemburg was really messy, not to speak of Trotsky.

I did try to be good. Every day, for example, I emptied the dishwasher. And a few times each day, I made coffee for H.

One day, however, when H. said that it was time to vacuum the house, I replied that the task might usefully wait until I was away somewhere doing a reading or teaching.

"Read the papers," H. said. "Away is a thing of the past."

It sounded like an accusation for a moment, and then, as H. gazed at me Gallically, it came to sound like a threat.

Soon the vacuum cleaner thundered through the house.

I loved days when we had nothing to do, with many days ahead the same, and we were like an elderly couple who had grown mellow and wise and could finish each other's paragraphs. Our only problem was that we couldn't agree on anything much.

We were happy in the lockdown, happier than we had been for a while. But I wished we could be happy in the easy, contented ways that the novelist and his boyfriend were happy and that other gay couples were happy.

I found a place in the garden to sit and read. Often, I remained outside as music blared from inside. House music, you could call it maybe; but also loud music.

One day, as I went inside, I found that H. was lifting the needle from a record. He was doing this, he said, because he did not want to annoy me with the music. I felt all sorry and tried to pretend the music did not, in fact, annoy me at all.

"Why don't you put it back on?" I asked.

For a second, and then two, I found the music exciting. My inner teenager woke up for a minute. The music was by Kraftwerk. I stopped and began to listen. I smiled in approval at H. I almost liked it, and then I made the mistake of attempting to dance to its rhythms.

The only thing I know about dancing comes from the film *Saturday Night Fever*, which I was forced to attend in 1978 when I had charge of a group of Spanish students in Dublin. I hated the film, and loathed it even more when a colleague, a crypto-semiotician, explained its inner workings to me in slow English.

But all I knew about dancing came from that film. Over the years, I had indeed hung out in discos, but I was more interested in back rooms, side glances, and full-frontal alcohol than in the niceties of dancing.

Nonetheless, I tried, as H. looked on. I moved my feet to the rhythm of the music and waved my arms around.

H. tried not to wince.

Quietly, like a guilty thing, I crept away. I felt like Mr. Jones in the song: "Something is happening here but you don't know what it is, do you, Mr. Jones?"

I understood that, rather than me mocking Kraftwerk, as I had been doing up to now, it was Kraftwerk mocking me.

"You are not cool enough to listen to us," whispered Kraftwerk.

In the garden, in a hammock hanging in a pomegranate tree, I read deep in Henry James.

• • •

We ordered bicycles online. I dreamed of us zooming through the suburban streets, passing the frightened bungalows, people cowering inside, zapping from channel to channel, hoping for redemption and washing their hands with prayerful zeal.

Through the window, they could, I imagined, see us freewheel by, like the cover image for some forgotten piece of vinyl.

A few days earlier than expected, the two bikes arrived. The only problem was that they needed to be assembled.

As H. began to study the manual, I tried to slip away. When he made clear that he would need me close by as he began the mammoth task, I insisted that I had urgent emails to send. But it was no use. He demanded that I stand there and look concerned as he lay on the ground and sweated and swore, asking God in heaven why the manufacturers had sent the wrong bolts and nuts, and not enough screws.

I imagined the online novelist, the happy one, sharing this task with his boyfriend, both in unison finding the right screws and realizing, as I did but H. did not, that the thin metal rods that H. said had been included by mistake had, in fact, been provided to stabilize the front wheels. I thought of Benjamin Britten, Gertrude Stein, Christopher Isherwood, and their partners. They would know how to look involved.

Since H. was in such a rage, not only against the bikes themselves and the factory that had made them but also against me, whose idea all of this was, I decided it was best to summon up a version of myself that I last used in school when I did not know why x equaled y.

I looked dumb, but sad and humble as well, mildly placid, but deeply engaged.

Soon, after much struggle and sighing, the bikes worked, and with helmets and masks on, we set out, flying down a hill with joy and glee and controlled abandon, like two men in an advertisement for posh soap.

It was years since I was on a bike. Something happened to my coiled-up spirit as I let the machine glide down Adelante to the beautifully named Easy Street and then to York and then to Marmion Way and then Arroyo Seco Park. When it was not downhill, it was flat. There was no traffic, and there were only some bewildered-looking pedestrians on the sidewalks, with masks on.

I did not know that a tributary of the L.A. River ran through the park and that it had a cycle lane on one of its banks. It was hard to use ordinary words about this so-called river. It is named the Arroyo Seco, which means "dry stream," and it is indeed dry, or dry enough, and it doesn't really have banks, since it is not really a river.

Los Angeles will be lovely when they finish it.

Even though it had recently rained, this fenced-off drain soon to join the river with the grandiose name still had no water. The L.A. River and its little tributary were in pain, I had always believed, calling out for mercy.

But now, as I nudged my bicycle onto the path, I felt that I had found some element of the city that had been hidden from me. No car could come here. No images of this strange, sad spectacle would ever be sent out into the world. There would be no: "Come to L.A.! Ride your bike by a river!" No one in their right mind would be here.

But it was almost beautiful. I should not have laughed at the L.A. River.

As I harbored these deep and liberating thoughts, H. sped by. When I looked behind, I saw the novelist and his partner, the happy ones, the online ones, in the form of ghosts, followed by all the happy homosexual pairs in history, cycling as best they could. I changed gear and moved farther ahead of them, following H., trying as best I could to catch up.

CLINICAL NOTES
BY LIZ MOORE

<u>March 12, 2020</u>

<u>Fact:</u> The baby has a fever.

> <u>Evidence:</u> Two thermometers produce a succession of worrisome readings. 103.9. 104.2. 104.8.

> <u>Evidence:</u> The baby is hot. The baby's cheeks are red. The baby is trembling. The baby, when he nurses, is nursing askew: mouth fluttering incorrectly, lips slack, hands and arms limp. The baby, instead of crying, is mewing.

<u>Fact:</u> Babies frequently get fevers.

> <u>Evidence:</u> Both of the babies in the household have gotten fevers regularly over the time that babies have resided in the household. Three years and nine months is the length of time that babies have resided in the household.

<u>Belief:</u> The 3.75-year-old does not have a fever.

Evidence: The 3.75-year-old's forehead is cool.

Methodology: The 3.75-year-old's mother tiptoes into her room, breath held, avoiding certain floorboards, lowering lips to skin, lips being the best fever-readers on the human body.

Question: What thermometer reading necessitates a visit to the pediatric emergency room?

Research Process: The baby's parents conduct several internet searches using the following phrases:
Pediatric temperature emergency room
104.8 fever E.R.

Answer: The internet returns two conflicting pieces of advice.
A.   *Go right now*
B.   *Give Tylenol; call doctor*

Response: The baby's parents look at each other silently for six seconds, considering more facts.

Fact: There is a new disease in the world.

Fact: It has entered the human population.

Fact: The baby's father was notified, yesterday, that three of his co-workers have this disease.

Acknowledgment: The timing looks bad.

> **Rebuttal:** Babies get fevers. Babies frequently get fevers. The baby has no other symptoms aside from a fever. Most fevers in babies are not caused by viruses that have recently entered the human population. The other three members of the baby's family do not, so far, show symptoms.

Unknowns: Infectiousness of virus. Disease course. Time from exposure to symptom manifestation. Typical expression of disease in adults and children. Short-term and long-term effects on both. Typical trajectory. Lethality.

Declaration: "There are a lot of unknowns here," the baby's mother says.

> **Considerations:** It's 1:45 in the morning. The baby's sister is asleep. One parent would have to drive the baby, alone, to the children's hospital. The other parent would—

Interruption: The baby vomits. The vomiting is matter-of-fact and unviolent. A bored opening of the mouth. The expulsion of the contents of the baby's stomach. Following the vomiting, the baby wilts. The baby falls asleep.

> **Considerations (cont.):** —have to stay behind with the baby's sister.

Further considerations: Is it a greater risk to take this baby into a medical setting than to monitor him at home? If what the baby has is not the new disease—could the baby or his parent actually get the new disease, from the medical setting?

Decision: The baby's parents choose Option B. Infant Tylenol is administered. At 1:50 a.m., the doctor is called.

Correction: It is not the doctor. It is the answering service. The doctor will call back.

Interlude: The parents clean the floor. They dim the lights in the living room. The father lies down on the sofa, baby on chest. The father notes the heat of the baby's body, improbable, heat like a kettle, an engine. Heat derived from work, from spent energy, the work of the new little body going to war. The father remembers the baby's first days, recalls swollen eyelids that opened and closed with real effort, underwater movements of fingers, considers how bodies of newborns are built like shields, the torso an inverted triangle, the limbs insubstantial. This thought reassures him. They are designed to survive, the father tells himself—an affirmation. The baby is 10 months old now. The baby has grown. His body is plump, his weight, on the chest of his father, both comfort and alarm, a reminder of all that has been invested into the baby's body (7,315 ounces of milk from the body of his mother, 722 raspberries, 480 ounces of yogurt, 120 bananas, 84 small pieces of cheese, 15 packets of small air-like food items called "yogurt melts," of which this baby is very fond, one taste of cake that the baby's sister furtively smuggled him), and aside from what's been physically invested into this baby's body, there is also the fact of their love for him. For his laugh. For the maw of his mouth, the three teeth the baby has sprouted, the way he has learned in the past week how to give a kiss, the way the kiss is deposited, open-mouthed, on the recipient's cheek—and the hand of the baby, which the father now touches, which the baby has recently learned how to wave. On his father's chest, all parts of the baby are still now. All parts of the father are still. The mother sits in a chair, watching them. Watching her phone. Awaiting the call of the doctor. Three times, she checks to ensure her phone is not set to silent.

Observation: An hour passes. The house is quiet. Maybe, thinks the baby's mother, it will all be—

> **Interruption:** The baby vomits. Onto the father's chest. The sofa. The rug. The baby lifts his head to observe what he's done. Lowers it directly into the pool of the liquid that has come out of his body. Returns to sleep.

Pause.

Command: "Take him," the baby's father says, quietly. "Take him."

Aftermath: The baby's mother takes the baby. Cleans him. The baby's father cleans his shirt, the sofa, the rug, his hair. Reclaims the baby.

Question: "What time is it?" the baby's father says.

Answer: It is 3:02 a.m.

Question: "Where the hell is this call?" the baby's father asks.

Decision: The mother, the milk-giver, will take the baby to the hospital. The father holds the baby, freshly changed, asleep, still smelling of bile. The mother packs a bag.

List: Into the bag go six diapers, one pack of wipes, two changes of clothes, two burp cloths—"take more," the father says, thinking of vomit—a manual breast pump, two bottles of pumped milk—in case of separation—an ice pack, one small soft cooler, water for the mother, trail mix for the mother, a phone charger for the mother's phone. The mother's phone. Her wallet. Her keys, which first drop to the ground with a clatter.

Interruption: The baby laughs.

Question: "Did he just laugh?" the mother asks.

Answer: He did. The baby has lifted his head. He gestures, open-palmed, toward the keys on the floor. I want. The baby smiles.

Observation: The baby's eyes are alert. The baby's color is better. The baby is looking around the room, making sounds with his mouth. "Ohwow, ohwow, ohwow," chants the baby, an expression of awe. His first words, which he recently learned.

Deduction: "He's better," the mother says. "Let's take his temperature again," the father says.

Result: 101.2.

Suggestion: "Maybe," the father says, "we can—"

Interruption: The phone rings. The doctor.

Advice: "She says we can wait until morning," the mother says.

Observation: The baby is rubbing his eyes. The baby looks tired.

Decision: The parents of the baby strip him to his diaper. Put him into a sleep sack, pink-trimmed, passed down from his sister. His housecoat, the mother calls it, remembering her grandmother's, remembering the candies her grandmother kept in its pockets, remembering the long tender feet of her grandmother, and the way she had of placing a hand on the back of the mother when she was ill, and the time she came and stayed with the mother when she had chicken pox as a child, watching *The Sound of Music* with her over and over again, never complaining or acting bored. And the thought of it moves her. All of those ancestors, all of that tenderness given to child after child, the last being this one—the baby she holds in her arms. As the mother remembers, she nurses the baby to sleep, tensing at every pause in his efforts, waiting for him to be sick again.

He isn't. For now, the mother will lay him down in his crib, in his pink housecoat, will watch as he sleeps, will lean down and place one hand to his forehead, testing again and again. Warm but not hot, she tells herself—though without the thermometer she cannot be certain. She lies down on the floor, next to the baby. Watches the baby. The baby is breathing. The baby is breathing. Dim light and shadow on the face of the baby. Through the slats of the crib, she touches one finger to the skin of the baby. Warm but not hot. Warm but not hot, she thinks—a chant, a prayer— though she cannot be certain.

THE ⟵ TEAM
BY TOMMY ORANGE

ou'd been staring at a wall in your office for what amount of time you weren't sure. Time slipped that way lately, as if behind a curtain, then back out again as something else, here as an internet hole, there as a walk on your street you insisted on calling a hike with your wife and son, here as a book your eyes look at, that you don't comprehend, there as crippling depression, here as observing circling turkey vultures, there as your ever-imminent anxiety, here as a failed Zoom call, there as a homeschooling shift with your son, here as April, May already gone, there as the obsession over the body count, the nameless numbers rising on endless graphics of animated maps. Time was not on your side or anyone's, it was dreaming its waste with you, as you, hidden and loud as the sun behind a cloud.

You were thinking of when you were last in public. This wasn't counting the masked and panicked weekly grocery-store runs, or the post-office-box scramble, you with your precariously stacked boxes of the unessential, keeping as much distance as you could from anyone you saw, especially after hearing a podcast that introduced you to the disgusting idea of mouth rain. You don't even make eye contact with anyone anymore, so afraid are you of the spread.

The last mass-gathering public-type thing you'd done was running your first half marathon. There's your medal in your office, hung like a deer head. A half marathon doesn't sound like a whole lot, it just being the half, but it was a big deal to you, to run and run for 13 miles without stopping. When you first started training, you actually paid money to join a running team that gathered together and pumped you up about how grueling it all was. You did chants and listened to your team leaders rant about their race times and the superior foods and energy sources they carried in plastic sacks around their waists. You hated the team training, so you quit and started to think of your whole body, and health, and routine, and running-songs playlist as the Team. You got up early to run, and you went on more than just one run a day sometimes. You kept to the mileage you planned, and kept to the diet prescribed by the app you downloaded to train—the app then was also part of the Team. The Team kept its promises to itself. The Team was your heart keeping healthy and your lungs keeping clear and your determination remaining determined to do this thing you decided you needed to do for reasons you don't even remember.

Running is surely as old as legs, and you'd been doing it yourself for quite a while, mostly to stave off the ever-encroaching pounds that come with age, but running to race was new, running for the distance, for a time, to cross the finish line, this was a strange kind of obligation you'd taken on, a mantle, a goal with a finish line. Running before modern times was serious business; it was running away or toward something with urgency, hunting, being hunted, or delivering a critical message. The first official marathon happened at the 1896 Olympics and was won by a Greek mailman. The race length was a nod to the ancient Greek legend of a runner who'd been running a message about victory just before collapsing and dying right then and there. There could be countless other examples of ancient running—surely Indians were running all over American countrysides before Cortés brought Iberian horses to Florida in 1519—and yet you are stuck with the image of the Indian on horseback, and when the image should represent Native people's sheer adaptability, it stands for the static, dead Indian. You've always known this image to reflect an aspect of you that was both true and not true, some kind of centaurian truth, because your dad is Native American, a Cheyenne Indian, and your mom is white, and both of them were runners, which is why you ever even thought to run in the first place, but regardless of ancient running and family heritage, and half-truths, there was no way to really know what kinds of running activities humans were up to since the beginning of legs.

After the race you went back up the mountain to where you moved when Oakland became a cost you couldn't afford five years ago. You went back up to isolation, and you were mostly safe from what others had to risk being together so closely in cities. But after the race, you were done running. The world came to a screeching halt, and so did your good feelings about it being a worthy endeavor, something worth working for. When the old white monsters at the top threw crumbs and ate heartily from the ridiculous plate that was the stimulus package, you felt the sick need to stop everything and watch it all burn, watch it lose its breath. With all the talking heads talking their talk, saying almost nothing, all you could do was watch, and it's all you did, all you felt you could do, which felt like doing something even though it was doing nothing, to watch, to listen, to read the news like something new might come of it more than new death, even while you thought the deaths could mean the old white monsters would suffer, but they didn't, and it turned out to be the same people who'd always suffered at the expense of the pigs having more than their fair share of the crop, slop to them because they didn't need it, a level of greed so beyond need you couldn't even conceptualize it. It was all in the name of freedom. You were taught that in school, and it was written in textbooks, the sanctimony of the free market, the Constitution and the Declaration of Independence, which referred and still refers to Indians as merciless savages.

The new Team was your family, the one you're at home with now. This was your wife, and your son, your sister-in-law and her two teenage girls. It was isolation itself, what you did with it, against it. The new Team was not running; it was planning meals together and sharing news of the outside world as read about and listened to from the inside of your insular lives, from the inside of your Bluetooth bass-heavy headphones. The new Team was the new future, which was yet to be determined, which seemed to be decided by individual communities and whether they believed in the number of lives lost and how it related to them. Your new Team was made up of frontline workers scanning your groceries and delivering your deliveries. It was made up of your old family, the one that had been broken up for so long it seemed absurd to even think of picking up the pieces, not to mention putting them back together. You were learning Cheyenne together, from your dad. It was his first language, and your sister had become fluent, and understanding a new language felt like something everyone needed to be thinking about, given that you'd lost the thread of truth, somewhere back when you thought you believed anymore in anything close to hope. Was it before Obama, or during Obama, or after Obama, this all was an important point in time to understand where you stood, what you understood to mean the future of the country, which flag you stood under, and what did it mean that white people were moving toward the minority—never mind hope, never mind prosperity, would you survive? No, you didn't run anymore, and it showed, and you showered maybe once a week, and forgot about your teeth. You drank too much, and smoked more cigarettes than ever. You would improve once things seemed to improve, once you got a glimmer of hope from the news; you're watching, something will come, a cure, a drop in numbers, a miracle drug, antibodies, something, anything else.

You're back at the wall, staring at it, unable to do anything but watch. It was the Teamwork being done by the whole new world, all those not directly affected, to watch and wait, to stay put, it would be a marathon, all this isolation, but it was the only way the Team could make it, humans, the whole damn race.

Translated by Sam Taylor from the French

One September evening, as the author Robert Broussard was giving a speech about his latest novel, someone threw a rock at his face. At the moment when the rock left the assailant's hand and began to fly through the air, the novelist was reaching the end of an anecdote that he had told many times before—about Tolstoy's being described as a "disgusting pig." To the author's disappointment, the audience reaction that night was no more than a smattering of polite laughter. He then leaned toward the glass of water on the table next to him, and so it was his left profile that the rock hit. The journalist who was interviewing him cried out in alarm, and soon the audience was yelling, too. In a panic, everyone ran from the room. Broussard was left alone, lying unconscious on the stage, blood pouring from his forehead.

When he came to, Robert Broussard was in a hospital bed, half his face covered with bandages. He wasn't in pain. He felt as if he were floating, and he would have liked that sensation of lightness to continue forever. He was a highly successful novelist, but his literary reputation was in inverse proportion to his sales figures. Ignored by the press, he was viewed contemptuously by his peers, who considered it laughable that Broussard should even call himself a writer. And yet he had a long backlist of bestsellers and a devoted fan base, made up mostly of women. Broussard's books never touched on religion or politics. He had no clear-cut opinions on anything. He did not confront issues such as gender or race, and he kept his distance from the controversies of the day. It came as a surprise that anyone would want to assault him.

A policeman interrogated him. He wanted to know if Broussard had any enemies. Did he owe anyone money? Was he sleeping with another man's wife? He asked lots of questions about women. Did Broussard have many affairs? With what kind of women? Could a jealous or rejected lover have slipped unnoticed into the audience? To all these questions, Robert Broussard responded with a shake of the head. Despite his dry mouth and the awful pain he had suddenly begun to feel in his eyeball, he described the nature of his existence to the policeman. He led a tranquil life, without any troubles or complications. Broussard had never been married and spent most of his time at his desk. He would sometimes eat dinner with friends from college, whom he'd known for 30 years, and on Sundays he went to his mother's house for lunch. "Nothing very exciting, I'm afraid," he concluded. The detective shut his notebook and left.

Broussard was now all over the news. Journalists fought

for an exclusive interview with him. Broussard was a hero. For some, he was a victim of a far-right vigilante; for others, a target of Islamic extremists. Some people believed that a bitter incel must have sneaked into the room that night, intent on punishing this man who had built his success on the mendacious myth of love. The famous literary critic Anton Ramowich published a five-page article on Broussard's work, which he had previously disdained. Ramowich claimed to have deciphered, between the lines of the author's light romantic novels, an acerbic critique of consumer society and a pointed analysis of social divisions. He labeled Broussard "the secret subversive."

After being discharged from the hospital, Broussard was invited to the Élysée Palace, where the French president, a busy, thin-faced man, acclaimed him as a war hero. "France is in your debt," he told the author. "France is proud of you." A bodyguard was sent to protect him: He visited Broussard's apartment and decided to cover the windows with paper and to move the entry phone to a different spot. The bodyguard was a stocky man with a shaved, shiny head, who told the novelist that he'd spent two months protecting a neo-Nazi pamphleteer who treated him like a servant and sent him to pick up his clothes from the dry cleaner's.

In the weeks that followed, Broussard was invited onto dozens of television shows, where the makeup artists took care to highlight the scar on his forehead. When he was asked if he regarded the attack on him as an assault on freedom of expression, his limp replies were taken as proof of modesty. For the first time in his life, Robert Broussard felt loved—and, even better, respected—by everyone around him. When he entered a room, with his black eye, his face like a wounded soldier's, an awed hush would fall in his wake. And his editor would put a hand on his shoulder, as proud as a horse breeder showing off his prize thoroughbred.

After a few months, the case was closed. No culprit was ever found: There was no camera in the bookstore where the speech was given, and the spectators had given conflicting accounts. On social media, the anonymous criminal became the object of excited speculation. An anarchist journalist, whose reputation was founded on the leaking of politicians' sex tapes, hailed the assailant as an icon of the invisible, forgotten masses. The nameless rock-thrower was the herald of a revolution. In daring to attack Broussard, he had fired the first shot against easy money, undeserved success, the capitalist media, and the tyranny of middle-aged white men.

The novelist's star waned. There were no more invitations to appear on television. His editor advised him to lie low and decided to delay the publication of his new novel. Broussard no longer dared Google himself. The things he read about himself were so full of hate that he found it hard to breathe. He felt his guts twist and drops of sweat trickle down his forehead. He returned to his tranquil, solitary life. One Sunday, after eating lunch with his mother, he decided to walk home. On the way, he thought about the book he wanted to write, the book that would solve everything.

A book that would put the chaos of the age into words, that would show the world the true Robert Broussard. He was thinking about all this when the first rock hit him. He didn't see where it came from, nor the ones that followed. He didn't even have time to cover his face with his hands. He just collapsed in the middle of the street, under a rain of stones.

IMPATIENT GRISELDA
BY MARGARET ATWOOD

D o you all have your comfort blankets? We tried to provide the right sizes. I am sorry some of them are washcloths—we ran out.

And your snacks? I regret that we could not arrange to have them cooked, as you call it, but the nourishment is more complete without this cooking that you do. If you put all of the snack into your ingestion apparatus—your, as you call it, mouth—the blood will not drip on the floor. That is what we do at home.

I regret that we do not have any snacks that are what you call vegan. We could not interpret this word.

You don't have to eat them if you don't want to.

Please stop whispering, at the back there. And stop whimpering, and take your thumb out of your mouth, Sir-Madam. You must set a good example to the children.

No, you are not the children, Madam-Sir. You are 42. Among us you would be the children, but you are not from our planet or even our galaxy. Thank you, Sir or Madam.

I use both because quite frankly I can't tell the difference. We do not have such limited arrangements on our planet.

Yes, I know I look like what you call an octopus, little

young entity. I have seen pictures of these amicable beings. If the way I appear truly disturbs you, you may close your eyes. It would allow you to pay better attention to the story, in any case.

No, you may not leave the quarantine room. The plague is out there. It would be too dangerous for you, though not for me. We do not have that type of microbe on our planet.

I am sorry there is no what you call a toilet. We ourselves utilize all ingested nourishment for fuel, so we have no need for such receptacles. We did order one what you call a toilet for you, but we are told there is a shortage. You could try out the window. It is a long way down, so please do not try to jump.

It's not fun for me, either, Madam-Sir. I was sent here as part of an intergalactical-crises aid package. I did not have a choice, being a mere entertainer and thus low in status. And this simultaneous translation device I have been issued is not the best quality. As we have already experienced together, you do not understand my jokes. But as you say, half an oblong wheat-flour product is better than none.

Now. The story.

I was told to tell you a story, and now I will tell you one. This story is an ancient Earth story, or so I understand. It is called "Impatient Griselda."

Once there were some twin sisters. They were of low status. Their names were Patient Griselda and Impatient Griselda. They were pleasing in appearance. They were

Madams and not Sirs. They were known as Pat and Imp. Griselda was what you call their last name.

Excuse me, Sir-Madam? Sir, you say? Yes?

No, there was not only one. There were two. Who is telling this story? I am. So there were two.

One day a rich person of high status, who was a Sir and a thing called a Duke, came riding by on a—came riding by, on a—if you have enough legs you don't have to do this riding by, but Sir had only two legs, like the rest of you. He saw Pat watering the—doing something outside the hovel in which she lived, and he said: "Come with me, Pat. People tell me I must get married so I can copulate legitimately and produce a little Duke." He was unable to just send out a pseudopod, you see.

A pseudopod, Madam. Or Sir. Surely you know what that is! You are an adult!

I will explain it later.

The Duke said: "I know you are of low status, Pat, but that is why I want to marry you rather than someone of high status. A high-status Madam would have ideas, but you have none. I can boss you around and humiliate you as much as I want, and you will feel so lowly that you won't say boo. Or boohoo. Or anything. And if you refuse me, I will have your head chopped off."

This was very alarming, so Patient Griselda said yes, and the Duke scooped her up onto his . . . I'm sorry, we don't have a word for that, so the translation device is of no help.

Onto his snack. Why are you all laughing? What do you think snacks do before they become snacks?

I shall continue the story, but I do counsel you not to annoy me unduly. Sometimes I get hangry. It means hunger makes me angry, or anger makes me hungry. One or the other. We do have a word for that in our language.

So, with the Duke holding on to Patient Griselda's attractive abdomen very tightly so she wouldn't fall off his—so she wouldn't fall off, they rode away to his palace.

Impatient Griselda had been listening behind the door. That Duke is a terrible person, she said to herself. And he is preparing to behave very badly to my beloved twin sister, Patient. I will disguise myself as a young Sir and get a job working in the Duke's vast food-preparation chamber so I can keep an eye on things.

So Impatient Griselda worked as what you call a scullery boy in the Duke's food-preparation chamber, where she or he witnessed all kinds of waste—fur and fect simply discarded, can you imagine that, and bones, after being boiled, tossed out as well—but he or she also heard all kinds of gossip. Much of the gossip was about how badly the Duke was treating his new Duchess. He was rude to her in public, he made her wear clothes that did not suit her, he knocked her around, and he told her that all the bad things he was doing to her were her own fault. But Patient never said boo.

Impatient Griselda was both dismayed and angry at this news. She or he arranged to meet Patient Griselda one day when she was moping in the garden, and revealed her true identity. The two of them performed an affectionate bodily gesture, and Impatient said, "How can you let him treat you like that?"

"A receptacle for drinking liquid that is half full is better than one that is half empty," Pat said. "I have two beautiful pseudopods. Anyway, he is testing my patience."

"In other words, he is seeing how far he can go," Imp said.

Pat sighed. "What choice do I have? He would not hesitate to kill me if I give him an excuse. If I say boo, he'll cut off my head. He's got the knife."

"We'll see about that," Imp said. "There are a lot of knives in the food-preparation chamber, and I have now had much practice in using them. Ask the Duke if he would do you the honor of meeting you for an evening stroll in this very garden, tonight."

"I am afraid to," Pat said. "He might consider this request the equivalent of saying boo."

"In that case, let's change clothes," Imp said. "And I will do it myself." So Imp put on the Duchess's robes and Pat put on the clothing of the scullery boy, and off they went to their separate places in the palace.

At dinner, the Duke announced to the supposed Pat that he had killed her two beautiful pseudopods, to which she said nothing. She knew in any case that he was bluffing, having heard from another scullery boy that the pseudopods had been spirited away to a safe location. Those in the food-preparation chamber always knew everything.

The Duke then added that the next day he was going

to kick Patient out of the palace naked—we do not have this naked on our planet, but I understand that here it is a shameful thing to be seen in public without your vestments. After everyone had jeered at Patience and wastefully pelted her with rotting snack parts, he said he intended to marry someone else, younger and prettier than Pat.

"As you wish, my lord," the supposed Patient said, "but first I have a surprise for you."

The Duke was already surprised simply to hear her speak.

"Indeed?" he said, curling his facial antennae.

"Yes, admired and always-right Sir," Imp said in a tone of voice that signaled a prelude to pseudopod excretion. "It is a special gift for you, in return for your great beneficence to me during our, alas, too short period of cohabitation. Please do me the honor of joining me in the garden this evening so we can have consolation sex once more, before I am deprived of your shining presence forever."

The Duke found this proposition both bold and piquant.

Piquant. It is one of your words. It means sticking a skewer into something. I am sorry I cannot explain it further. It is an Earth word, after all, not a word from my language. You will have to ask around.

"That is bold and piquant," the Duke said. "I'd always thought you were a dishrag and a doormat, but now it seems, underneath that whey face of yours, you are a slut, a trollop, a dolly-mop, a tart, a floozy, a tramp, a hussy, and a whore."

Yes, Madam-Sir, there are indeed a lot of words like that in your language.

"I agree, my lord," Imp said. "I would never contradict you."

"I shall see you in the garden after the sun has set," the Duke said. This was going to be more fun than usual, he thought. Maybe his soi-disant wife would show a little action for a change, instead of just lying there like a plank.

Imp went off to seek the scullery boy, namely Pat. Together they selected a long, sharp knife. Imp hid it in her brocaded sleeve, and Pat concealed herself behind a shrub.

"Well met by moonlight, my lord," Imp said when the Duke appeared in the shadows, already unbuttoning that portion of his clothing behind which his organ of pleasure was habitually concealed. I have not understood this part of the story very well, since on our planet the organ of pleasure is located behind the ear and is always in plain view. This makes things far easier, as we can see for ourselves whether attraction has been generated and reciprocated.

"Take off your gown or I'll rip it off, whore," the Duke said.

"With pleasure, my lord," Imp said. Approaching him with a smile, she drew the knife from her richly ornamented sleeve and cut his throat, as she had cut the throat of many a snack during the course of her scullery-boy labors. He uttered barely a grunt. Then the two sisters performed an act of bodily affection, and then they ate the Duke all up—bones, brocaded robes, and all.

Excuse me? What is WTF? Sorry, I don't understand.

Yes, Madam-Sir, I admit that this was a cross-cultural

moment. I was simply saying what I myself would have done in their place. But storytelling does help us understand one another across our social and historical and evolutionary chasms, don't you think?

After that, the twin sisters located the two beautiful pseudopods, and there was a joyful reunion, and they all lived happily in the palace. A few suspicious relatives of the Duke came sniffing around, but the sisters ate them too.

The end.

Speak up, Sir-Madam. You didn't like this ending? It is not the usual one? Then which ending do you prefer?

Oh. No, I believe that ending is for a different story. Not one that interests me. I would tell that one badly. But I have told this one well, I believe—well enough to hold your attention, you must admit.

You even stopped whimpering. That is just as well, as the whimpering was very irritating, not to mention tempting. On my planet, only snacks whimper. Those who are not snacks do not whimper.

Now, you must excuse me. I have several other quarantined groups on my list, and it is my job to help them pass the time, as I have helped you pass it. Yes, Madam-Sir, it would have passed anyway, but it would not have passed so quickly.

Now I'll just ooze out underneath the door. It is so useful not to have a skeleton. Indeed, Sir-Madam, I hope the plague will be over soon, too. Then I can get back to my normal life.

UNDER THE MAGNOLIA
BY YIYUN LI

he couple had arranged to meet Chrissy near the Battle Monument. She had met them once, five years ago, when she served as the buyers' lawyer at the closing of their house. Soon after, the wife contacted her about estate planning. Chrissy sent them material and never heard back. She had forgotten them until the wife emailed again, apologizing for having disappeared. "We've set our hearts to follow through this time," she wrote.

They were not the first procrastinating clients. People told Chrissy about the distress of appointing guardians for their infant children, of making decisions for their future selves. She herself had neither a will nor plans in place—nothing wrong with that. A doctor could smoke or, like her father, drink himself to oblivion. No one says you have to live up to the standard defined by your profession.

The magnolia trees lining the avenue were at their peak. Chrissy picked up a palm-size petal on a bench. Magnolias are such confident flowers. The petals, even fallen, feel alive.

Years ago Chrissy and her two best friends dug a hole

and buried an envelope under one of those magnolia trees. Inside they had written notes, to be read again when they turned 50. To mark the solemnity of the event, they each put a single earring in it. Chrissy's was an opal unicorn.

None of them remembered the envelope when they turned 50. The memory only came back to Chrissy now.

"Jeannie?" a man a few steps away said tentatively.

Chrissy said she was not Jeannie, and he apologized. Was he meeting Jeannie for a date? They would have to take their masks off, she thought, to make a good impression. And how could they trust each other if they took off their masks?

The couple had no trouble recognizing Chrissy, nor she them. They were the only three people near the sculpture of General Washington. The couple apologized that their two friends, the witnesses, were running late.

Chrissy preferred punctuality. She disliked small talk. Still, she asked the couple about their life under lockdown. The husband nodded courteously and strolled away. He probably hated small talk, too.

"And the children? Which grades are they in now?" Chrissy said.

The wife glanced at the husband. He was farther away, studying General Washington. "Ethan is in sixth grade." There was a pause before that answer came.

Did they have one child? Chrissy remembered two, from the small talk five years ago. But it was true that only

Ethan's name was in the wills. Perhaps she had mixed them up with another family.

"You must be thinking of . . . Zoe?" the wife said in a lowered voice.

"Right . . . ," Chrissy said. She knew then what the wife would say, and was relieved that the witnesses arrived just then. Zoe was dead. Chrissy wished she had not asked about the children. Such an innocent question, but there was never a truly innocent question.

The signing took no more than 10 minutes. The couple was healthy. Neither had been married before, or had children outside this marriage. No complications, that was how Chrissy thought of clients like them. Yet they all came with some complications. Often Chrissy preferred not to dwell upon them.

As the couple and the witnesses walked away, Chrissy called out to the wife: "Mrs. Carson."

The husband and the witnesses walked on, in a triangular formation with the right distance in between. Chrissy wanted to say something about Zoe. The wife had mentioned the name for a reason.

The wife gestured to the papers in Chrissy's folder. "Strangely uplifting, isn't it? Signing our wills on a sunny day like this."

"It's a good thing to do," Chrissy said, an automatic response.

"Yes," the wife said, and thanked Chrissy again.

They would part then, and they might not see each other again. Chrissy would forget this meeting, as she had forgotten what she wrote to herself as a teenager. But someday she would remember this moment, and she wished that she had said more than a platitude, as she wished she had remembered the note to herself, or she had said something to her father about his drinking.

"I'm so sorry," Chrissy said, "about Zoe." The most banal words, but there are never the right words. That's an excuse for saying nothing.

The wife nodded. "Sometimes I wish Zoe had been less resolute," she said. "I wish she had been like me or her father. We're both procrastinators."

And yet no teacher or parent would encourage a child's procrastination or indecision, Chrissy thought. Why did she and her friends believe that decades later, they would still remember the notes, and they would still be interested in them? The confidence in life's consistency, for a young person, easily turns into the despair at life's unchangeableness.

"But you've followed through this time," Chrissy said, pointing to the folder. A platitude again, but platitudes, like procrastination, have their meaning, too.

OUTSIDE
BY ETGAR KERET

Translated by Jessica Cohen from the Hebrew

hree days after the curfew was lifted, it was clear that no one was planning to leave home. For reasons unknown, people preferred to stay inside, alone or with their families, perhaps simply happy to keep away from everyone else. After spending so much time indoors, everyone was used to it by now: not going to work, not going to the mall, not meeting a friend for coffee, not getting an unexpected and unwanted hug on the street from someone you took a yoga class with.

The government allowed a few more days to adapt, but when it became obvious that things weren't going to change, they had no choice. Police and army forces began knocking on doors and ordering people out.

After 120 days of isolation, it's not always easy to remember what exactly you used to do for a living. And it's not as if you're not trying. It was definitely something involving a lot of angry people who had trouble with authority. A school, perhaps? Or a prison? You have a vague memory of a skinny kid just sprouting a mustache throwing a stone at you. Were you a social worker in a group home?

You stand on the sidewalk outside your building, and the soldiers who walked you out signal for you to start moving. So you do. But you're not sure exactly where you're headed. You scroll through your phone for something that might help you get things straight. Previous appointments, missed calls, addresses in your memos. People rush past you on the street, and some of them look genuinely panicked. They can't remember where they're supposed to go, either, and if they can, they no longer know how to get there or what exactly to do on the way.

You're dying for a cigarette, but you left yours at home. When the soldiers barged in and yelled at you to leave, you barely had time to grab your keys and wallet, even forgetting your sunglasses. You could try to get back inside, but the soldiers are still around, impatiently banging on your neighbors' doors. So you walk to the corner store and find you have nothing but a five-shekel coin in your wallet. The tall young man at the checkout, who reeks of sweat, snatches the cigarette pack he just handed you: "I'll keep it for you here." When you ask if you can pay with a credit card, he grins as if you just told him a joke. His hand touched yours when he took the cigarettes back, and it was hairy, like a rat. A hundred twenty days have passed since someone last touched you.

Your heart pounds, the air whistles through your lungs, and you're not sure if you're going to make it. Near the

ATM sits a man wearing dirty clothes, and there's a tin cup next to him. You do remember what you're supposed to do in this situation. You quickly walk past him, and when he tells you in a cracked voice that he hasn't eaten anything in two days, you look in the opposite direction, avoiding eye contact like a pro. There's nothing to be afraid of. It's like riding a bike: The body remembers everything, and the heart that softened while you were alone will harden back up in no time.

KEEPSAKES
BY ANDREW O'HAGAN

ofty Brogan worked as a fishmonger in the Salt-market. People said he was the fastest skinner in Glasgow, but he couldn't do jokes like the other guys. This manic lady came to the stall every morning and told them she wanted kippers. "I'm Geetha from Parnie Street," she said on that particular day. "And my name means 'song.'"

"You're in the right place," Elaine the boss said. "Lofty here's a lovely singer, aren't you, darling?" He wrapped the kippers in some greaseproof paper. The boss had lipstick on her teeth. "Come on, Geetha," she went on to say, "why don't you change it up a bit today? We've got all the stuff here for a fish stew."

"Cacciucco," Lofty said.

"Red mullet. A bit of sole. Clams."

"I can't cope with fancy fish," Geetha said.

Elaine told her she was making a mistake. "You're a great cook, and you're going to turn into a kipper if you eat any more."

Geetha opened her purse and picked out the usual amount.

"She used to run the best Indian restaurant in Argyle

Street," Elaine said when the lady walked off with her bag. "I feel sorry for her."

There was too much history, Lofty thought. He was OK working at the Fish Plaice, but it wasn't his trade. He'd served his time as a joiner. He liked Elaine, that was all, and building sites were a nightmare. The main thing he cared about was European cities. He saved up all his spare cash so that he could fly off to these places, the emptier the better. At work, he hardly spoke. He knew about mussels and whelks, how long to cook a John Dory, and he got nice looks over the iceboxes. Elaine called him Angel Eyes. The market did poultry as well as fish, and he could sell squabs as fast as he could sell an octopus, so she had no complaints. Some things he said, his work mates didn't get. The day before the lockdown, he combed his blond hair into a quiff and wrote an ad for a boyfriend. Elaine was excited about the ad, but he told her it was no big deal, just a dating profile. "You're nice-looking, Lofty," she said to him during the break, "and tall. You should've stuck in at school. That way you wouldn't be renting rooms and paying these extortionate rents."

"You took all the houses. All the prospects." Elaine was standing under a sign that said "Want Fresher Fish? Buy a Boat."

"What you on about?"

"You seniors," Lofty said. "And now we're stuck."

"I'll seniors you," she said, before adding something about his mother. "An educated woman like that. How'd you get to be so spoiled?"

"Oh, yeah," he said. "Totally spoiled. We've had two 'once in a generation' crises in a dozen years. Spoiled rotten."

The pet shop closed the next morning. The guy never sold anything anyway: The animals were just his pals. But he said he'd watched *Newsnight* and everybody was going into quarantine, so, against the rules, he released his canaries on Glasgow Green. "Oh, my God," Lofty said, "are you tipping your goldfish into the Clyde?" Next door to Pet Emporium, the Empire Bar hung on until lunchtime, then closed. By the end of the week, the street was deserted and nothing was happening on Grindr. The flat Lofty rented looked down on the Green, and it was strange for him to see that nobody was outside the courthouse. The smoke from the Polmadie furnace had stopped dead.

He didn't like calling his mother. Half the time she'd just talk about the past or go on about money. "You're addicted to being awkward," she said to him that afternoon. "Nothing's ever your fault."

"What?"

"It must be such a comfort."

"My life is a result of your decisions."

"Oh, get a grip. You're twenty-seven years old."

"I didn't want to be a joiner. I didn't think I'd stay at the market."

"You're always late to the party," she said. "Why not throw your own party? Why not fill it with people you care about and show some commitment?"

"Because you drank all the Champagne," he said.

He didn't call her for another 10 days, and when he did a nurse answered. She said that his mother couldn't come to the phone, that things were pretty bad, and later that day they took her in an ambulance to the Royal Infirmary. It ended very quickly after that. There was nothing he could do, and then it was too late to do anything. A doctor had called his older brother in London, who then rang Lofty, but he wouldn't pick up. Daniel had been nothing to him for years—Dan was away. Dan was out of it.

They had a spat when their father died in 2015. Lofty accused his brother of stealing a briefcase from their parents' flat. "That's the maddest accusation I've ever heard," Dan texted him at the time, but Lofty just ignored it. Then Dan ranted and raved to their mother, before blocking him, which made Lofty feel victorious. It was obvious Dan was guilty and out of control, not only about the theft but about everything. Dan had always acted as if his family was a total drain on his concentration. The one time Lofty went to see him, they nearly had a fight in the middle of Notting Hill Gate. After drinking at a private club, Dan started shouting in the street about Lofty being "toxic and self-righteous, unreachably angry." Whatever. Lofty spat on the ground right next to him.

"Your life is a joke, Dan. All this cash. You make me sick." Their mother later told Lofty she'd heard about the argument. He knew that she and his brother agreed: It was Lofty who had the problem. They were "on the same page," or into the same books. They used words like "dysfunctional." People had "issues." After the thing with the briefcase, his mother sent him a book in the post called *How to Be Free of Yourself.* Lofty never worked out if she took him seriously about the theft. She never brought it up, not once. He felt detached in a whole new way and was tearful as he left his flat, banging the door. He carried the toolbox down the stairs and thought of it as doing weights.

It would take an hour to get to her place. In the Saltmarket, all the shutters were down. The virus was like a revolution in the brain, like a brand-new argument. A man was slumped outside the Old Ship Bank pub with his head between his knees. Lofty passed the solicitors' office and looked up at No. 175. His father had been obsessed with tales of their Irish ancestors—including a few young footballers who were among the first to play for Glasgow Celtic, Molly Brogan, who sold flowers at St. Enoch's, the prizefighters, the shebeeners, and the first Alexander Brogan, a part-time chemist who poisoned his wife. They'd all lived there, "the five Alexanders." The first came from Derry in 1848 and went straight from the ship to the Parish Relief. Lofty stood back in the middle of the road. It said "1887" at the top of the crow-stepped gable, and he realized the building must've replaced an older one. The Brogans: up there with their Papist utensils and their strong views about how to survive.

He crossed the river and went up Victoria Road. He noticed the post office was still open. He looked at his watch. The removal guy said they would do it quickly and maintain social distancing and be out of the flat by two o'clock. How did people keep their distance while carrying a three-piece suite? He changed hands; the toolbox was heavy. He reached the park and suddenly felt he should sit down on a bench. After taking out his phone, he swiped for a bit. "No, no, nope," he said. "Not with that face." He went onto Instagram and posted a selfie with the trees behind him. Within minutes, Elaine had "liked" it and posted a comment, two thumbs and a love heart.

He blocked her, then lit a cigarette, then deleted his account. A policeman got out of a van and walked over to a group of schoolgirls sitting on the grass. "What's your plans?" he heard the officer saying.

"Just sitting," one of them said.

"It's time to move on, I'm afraid."

"That's right! It's not your grass!" Lofty shouted. He stood up and the officer looked at him and the girls giggled.

"Are you OK, sir?" the policeman asked.

He walked away with the heavy toolbox. It was the only thing his father had left him, the toolbox and the stuff inside.

There were ferns in her front garden. The key was under a brick. He unlocked the storm doors and saw the hall was pretty empty, except for an unplugged telephone in the corner and personal things here and there, framed certificates in boxes. It was a small flat, perfectly proportioned, with tiled fireplaces in the living room and both bedrooms. There was a shadow on the carpets where the beds had been; the sofa was gone, plus the dining table, the TV, all her side tables, rugs, and lamps. He wasn't keeping any of it. He'd told the guys to take it all away and do what they liked with it. In the corner of the kitchen, he found a wooden stool he remembered from childhood that his mother painted with blue gloss. He opened the toolbox and took out a hacksaw, pausing to replace the blade. He cut up the stool and then he found some newspaper. He lit a fire in the living room. At one point he had three fires going—one in each room. He started emptying the bags. He would let one fire die down while building another, using a shovel to scoop the hot ashes into a bucket he'd found in the backcourt. Late in the evening, he found bottles from her departed drinks trolley and drank Pernod by the neck. He put the other bottles out. In one of the bags in the hall he found a long dripping string of rosary beads. God knows how many buckets he took outside, but there was a heap of ashes cooling in the backcourt. It must have been midnight when he put a coil of TV cables into the living room fire, an old telephone directory, and then he opened the last of the black bin bags and found it—the briefcase.

He sat cross-legged and opened it, the fire leaping beside him and bouncing shadows around the room. "Who, Me?" it said on a leaflet, the first of many inside the briefcase from Alcoholics Anonymous. He read each one and slugged the Pernod. He found a series of postcards from Oban—the old man's solo holiday destination—and in each one he went on about the weather before he signed off, "with love." Lofty worried he might be like him but enjoyed the way the postcards turned the flame green. In a zipped compartment he found letters and birth certificates going back years, and a school photograph with different writing on the back: "Alexander and Daniel, St. Ninians, 1989." He looked at his brother's face and knew for a certainty that he'd never see him again.

He took a Stanley knife and cut the soft leather into strips. The smell of it burning gave a whole new feel to his mother's front room. Eventually there was nothing much left, the wooden frames had all crackled away, and he'd twisted the screws out of the walls with pliers and tossed them into the bucket. Eventually, in the middle of the night, he took a scraper and removed layers of wallpaper. The last layer before the plaster was pink with white flowers, and he threw bunches of it into the fire. He decided he would wait for all the ashes in the backcourt to become cold, and then he'd put a load of them into the empty toolbox, go to the post office in the morning, and post it to Daniel's London address. It was the least he could do. About 4:00 a.m. he could hear birds chirping loudly in the street.

He took out his father's favorite chisel. It had a faded stamp on the metal part—"J. Tyzackand Son, Sheffield, 1879." He put it in the fire and then walked to the living room window. It didn't matter that the steel would be left over. He felt he had done his best. There was music outside. The lights in people's flats seemed bright at that hour, and he wondered if everyone was up. Here and there, remains had gone from houses or care homes without funerals or anything. "I wonder if she knew," he said. Then he placed his hands on the cold glass and thought of Malmo in the spring.

THE GIRL WITH THE BIG RED SUITCASE BY RACHEL KUSHNER

n that old tale by Poe, they locked out the commoners and locked in the plague, the uninvited guest to their costume ball. Their mistake is a lesson for the reader only, since the highborn fools in the story all die. I've read the tale, taken the lesson. And yet, here I am in a walled castle and with a small group of people I might describe, if pressed, as dissolute snobs.

This was an accident. I got here well before refrigerated trucks idled outside the municipal morgue, down the road. When I arrived in this country, life remained fairly normal. The virus was not close. I "felt sorry" for the people of Wuhan and continued with my own plans, as an author doing frivolous author-y things, like visiting a castle where I'd been invited for a week's stay, alongside people whose sole commonality was to pretend these kinds of bizarre sinecures are normal. I'd brought young Alex, who inspires wrestling matches among dowagers competing to have him at their brunch. His beauty is of a dissident, orphaned hue. Or darker. He looks, in fact, a lot like Dzhokhar Tsarnaev, but I promise he has bombed nothing except a few social occasions to which he arrived unfashionably late.

We were waiting it out, this mess that no person on Earth will escape. At first, to cozen our own distress, Alex and I treated our castlemates as bad objects of amusement. We poked fun at the Charlemagne biographer and the pajama-like "house master's" robe he wore to dinner, his obsession with the Duke of Wellington, with dueling, with all manner of what Alex summarized as post-Napoleonic torpor. We derided the journalist who believed anyone left of center was on Putin's payroll, this mythic payroll, so insidious we almost wondered if we were on it ourselves. And we laughed at the Norwegian author for the fact that he was, we were told, the most important author in Scandinavia, and yet, unlike all other Scandinavians, this extremely important and famous man didn't speak even a single word of English. He gathered with the rest of us but contributed only an air of dazed elsewhereness, seemingly unconcerned with the arch Anglo-banter that ricocheted around him. We never laughed at his wife, who translated for him, as some women do even for men who speak the language. She shared none of her own thoughts, this handsome woman with an indeterminate European accent, and instead sat on the terrace, smoking and silently watching the rest of us cheapen the air with our opinions.

As reality set in that we were stuck here, they became like relatives, people you didn't choose but must love. The Charlemagne biographer's habit of referring to Alex as Homo Juvenilis became a trend. I was working on a novel about early humans, and the biographer would quiz me nightly on my latest thoughts in regard to my Homo Primitivo, as if it were a creature I was keeping in my room. We now admired the Norwegian's refusal of English, of Anglo-superdominance, like a monk's rejection of intimate congress and a Luddite's of looms. We accepted the journalist's ritual invocation of Putin at dinner as one might an empty chair for Elijah. When the Charlemagne biographer suggested we each hold court with a story, and that it be not about the sickness, sadness, and death that had afflicted this region, and instead a happy tale, we agreed. Tonight it was the Norwegian's turn.

"My story is about a man named Johan," the Norwegian said in his language, and his wife repeated in English.

This was after dinner, which took place in a small room with an enormous table, its low ceiling greased and blackened by chimney smoke. The Norwegian told his story in fragments, to give his wife time to translate. As she spoke his words to us, he gazed off, introspective, his triangle of puffy gray hair aiming in two directions like divergent philosophies.

"I knew Johan through some university friends in Oslo. He had planned to move to Prague in the summer of 1993. Prague, then, attracted a certain type—people like Johan, college-educated layabouts without concrete aspirations who talked about wanting to 'open a literary space' or 'start a magazine' but mostly sat around feeling that life had little point. These types, which Johan perfectly illustrated, were moody and average-looking young men—and I should be an expert on them, as I was one myself—depressives who lacked purpose but who, in the interim of locating one, slept late and read a lot of film criticism and French theory, and brooded over unobtainable women who burned into their field of vision. In failing to capture them, these unemployed men with a lot of free time felt greatly persecuted, which they took out on the somewhat homelier females who made themselves earnestly available."

After translating this part, the wife and husband spoke in Norwegian to each other, as if working something out, about this story and what he would tell. We could see between them that he was the type he described, disgruntled, and with clumsy features, while the wife possessed that kind of beauty that seems like a form of cleverness, something she's figured out that the rest of us haven't.

"These men who didn't know what to do with their lives, and only loved women who brutally ignored them, suffered from a general inertia they blamed on Oslo instead of themselves. Prague, and its opening to the West, the excitement of the Velvet Revolution, of cheap rent and a bohemian scene featuring superior and more obliging women, took on promise as a solution to poor character, to failure at life. Johan had a friend who was teaching at a film school there and invited him to come and stay. There was a going-away party that I myself attended, and then Johan took off for his new life. We were all a little begrudging. If he failed, we'd gloat. If he succeeded, maybe we, too, would move to Prague.

"Johan arrived at that city's airport on a cold and rainy Sunday morning. Nonresidents lined up, nothing out of the ordinary, Johan among them, excited for this new chapter, as the line inched forward to the rhythmic stamping of documents. When it was his turn to present his passport, the trouble began.

"The immigration officer demanded to know why Johan's passport was wrinkled, the photo water-damaged.

"'It's still an official document,' Johan explained to the officer, who remained as blank and steely as a military tank. 'It's just a bit worn because I spilled something on it a while back.'

"At the other passport kiosks, stamps ka-junked and people sailed through, without interrogation or arguing, one after another, while Johan went in circles with the border agent.

"Eventually he was taken to a small room with a reinforced door that was locked (he tried it), and left there for several hours. He began to understand, staring at the blank, reinforced door, that there was an iron fist under the velvet curtain, or however the expression went.

"In the late afternoon, another man, as rude and dispassionate as the first, came in and asked him a series of questions. Johan answered and 'tried not to be a dick,' as he later put it. He was left in the room again. It was evening before the same man came back and told Johan he would not be admitted to the country unless a representative from the Norwegian Consulate was willing to intervene and issue him a new passport. Johan was allowed to place a call to the consulate. One phone call, they said, as if he were guilty of something. Seeing as it was Sunday, the consulate was closed.

"Johan was taken back to the long border-control hallway. The agent informed him he would remain there until the next day. If the consulate agreed to help him, he could gain entry. If not, they would force him onto a flight home.

"It was late, and the hall was empty, the kiosks locked and dark. The other travelers had all gone on to unseen realities that Johan, trapped alone in this bleak interstice, envied. He sat in a chair. He was thirsty and had no water. He had no cigarettes. He was cold and had no jacket. He was trying to 'lie down' in the chair, his neck resting on the hard edge of the seat back, wondering if he could sleep this way, when he heard a loud bang.

"At the other end of the hall was a young woman. She'd dropped a large red suitcase on the floor. Johan watched as she opened it and riffled through. She located cigarettes and lit one. Kneeling on the floor with the lit cigarette in her mouth, she proceeded to reorganize her suitcase, her busy movements those of someone free of worry, killing time. Periodically, she got up and paced around.

"How did she have such energy? Johan had to focus his energy on his outrage at being detained.

"She waved at him. He waved back. She walked down to his end of the hall and offered him a cigarette.

"Up close, he saw that she was way beyond his league:

in other words, exactly his type, this confident girl in tight jeans and white high-top Converses. Later, he held on to details. The jeans. The high-tops.

"'Why do they keep you?' she asked in stilted English.

"'They don't like my passport,' he said. 'What about you?'

"She smiled and said, 'I guess you could say they don't like my passport either.'

"He asked where she was from. Her answer, the way she said the word, became another detail he held tight. 'Yugo-slavia.'

"Johan understood it was possible she had no passport for them to like or dislike, just as there was no Yugoslavia. Not anymore.

"She was trying to go to Abu Dhabi, she said. Johan nodded, unable to remember if that was the Emirates or Qatar or where. He saw oil sheikhs and girls like this one. He wanted to ask questions, but all he could think of was Who are you, which you never ask, and no one can answer.

"She went back to her end of the hall. He smoked the cigarette as if inhaling the mystery of this brazen, sexy girl. He was pondering going down to speak with her when border agents came into the hall and approached her. There was a discussion that Johan could not hear, the girl nodding, not saying much. She was escorted out, dragging her big red suitcase.

"Johan slept badly, upright, in the uncomfortable chair. When he woke, it was dawn. Rain fell over the tarmac beyond the windows in cruel sheets."

• • •

"Johan's dealing with the consulate, and the period in which he bummed around Prague, is not of interest to our story. He was there for a while and then home. He continued to think of that night at passport control, of the girl and her brave and casual boredom. He graded himself an F in enduring a taste of repressive Soviet-style authority. An F for failing to learn more about the girl when he had his chance.

"Back in Oslo, Johan was hired in the first wave of the dot-com industry, sold his stake in a 'start-up'—whatever that is—and made good money. He could afford to travel and avoid working for a while. He decided to go to Abu Dhabi, to try to find the girl.

"He'd read about women from poor and war-ravaged countries who immigrated there by arrangement with bad people who forced the women into prostitution. Johan felt certain the girl he met had come deliberately, knowingly, to hustle in an oil-rich nation. She grew larger in his mind.

"He spent two weeks searching, night after night, in the various hooker establishments of Abu Dhabi, neobrutalist hotels with loud, smoky mezzanines, as he scanned the faces of women who scanned him as a mark. He watched women exit elevators and click through hotel lobbies, or stand around in lounges, preening and alert. His conversations usually ended in misunderstanding; the women all thought he was looking for a type, not a specific actual person. Or they played games, tossed false leads. Sure, I know her. Blond, yes? She'll be here later. Or, I'll arrange a party and you can see her. Or, You'll forget all about her, trust me.

"Only once did the offer seem worth pursuing. A dark-haired woman with large eyes and a crooked nose spoke to Johan in a frank way that he read as believable. I know this girl you mean. She's Croatian. Me, I'm Croatian. She came here around then, yes. I think she told me about that, some trouble when she arrived. Yes, she's still here.

"That night, he went to the small, dingy club where the girl with the crooked nose said to meet. She was there with another girl who was tall and blond. Her hair wasn't long, as he recalled, but short and bleached almost white. He told her his story, that he'd seen a girl—maybe her—in the air-port trying to enter Prague three years earlier.

"'I don't remember you,' she said. 'But I think that was me.'

"'Did you have a giant red suitcase?' he asked.

"'Yes, I did.'

"It was her, and of course she would not remember him. She was not going to be weighted by sentimental memories of a dweeb like Johan. He remembered her, and that was enough.

"For the next week, Johan saw her every night, and every night, he paid for her company. He had planned to dem-onstrate his interest, his sincerity, by insisting they merely talk, get to know each other, despite the money he was spending. But that was not how things went. She seemed to prefer the exchange of services that she was used to, and

Johan went along with it, perhaps too easily. This caused him guilt and confusion. But after several days together in this stilted arrangement, something shifted. She turned to him, you could say. I still don't understand it. It's baffling, but she fell in love with Johan."

There was a pause in the story while the Norwegian and his wife spoke in their language. The wife's tone was corrective.

"She wants me to here acknowledge," she translated for him, speaking of herself in the third person, "that no one understands why anyone falls in love. And that my surprise that she did fall in love, instead of use him, probably derives from a cheap stereotype that post-bloc Slavic women are cynical and calculating. My wife is right. I should not be surprised the girl had a heart, and that she could find something to love in Johan, even if I don't. I'm a lot like him, as I said, and we are, in truth, adversaries to a degree. But let us continue.

"This girl moved to Oslo with Johan. The first few months, for him anyhow—we can't speak for her—were blissful. The person he'd fantasized about for three long years was funny and charming. His friends all liked her. She adapted easily, and even took it upon herself to learn Norwegian.

"But as they settled into life together, doubt crept in for Johan. If he went out alone, she'd ask where he'd been. Occasionally, when they passed other women on the street, part of him peeled off, dreamed of strangers. One morning she turned to him in bed and her breath, morning rank, singed his nostrils like a moral failing. All he could do was hold his own breath.

"He started to become annoyed when she didn't know a particular band, a movie. Since he'd spent his early 20s slacking and absorbing culture while she was fleeing a failed state, he was impatient with her ignorance of what mattered to him.

"She began to want sex with Johan more than he wanted it with her. That it was always available to him devalued it to a degree he'd never imagined possible. It was like walking through a room constantly filled with steaming piles of food and you really just want a break from food. He wanted a break from her.

"He suggested she visit her mother, who lived in Zagreb. It was while she was away that he began to suspect she was not, perhaps had never been, the heroic creature in the airport with the white high-tops. They don't like my passport either. He was riven by nostalgia for that girl. Because this one, it wasn't her. Even if it was her it wasn't her. What he'd seen, wanted, extolled, was not the girl he'd found. She wasn't heroic. She was normal, needy, imperfect. The relationship, as far as he was concerned, was over.

"Johan was too cowardly to tell her in person. When she returned from her mother's, he'd left her a note. He said he'd be gone a few days while she sorted out what to do and where to go. Johan took a train to Sweden. He sat in an ugly hotel bar with brash Swedes and drank flat, tasteless beer and felt depression spreading through his body. It was wintertime and bleak. The girl he'd dreamed of was nowhere to be found. This plunged him into existential crisis. He stared out the window at the heavy sky and bare trees, which had tattered plastic bags caught in their branches."

The Norwegian sighed audibly and looked around the table, as if for a reaction. His wife was also quiet.

We were all confused. This was it?

"But, but but," the Charlemagne biographer said, "what about a happy ending? That was the rule."

"It is a happy ending," the Norwegian said in his language, and his wife repeated in ours.

"Of sad Johan drinking flat beer in a tacky bar, loveless and alone?"

"The story is happy for me," the Norwegian said, "not for Johan."

"Oh? And why is that?"

"Because I married the woman he was looking for. And she is telling you this story now."

We all looked at his wife.

"My husband has had his fun," she said, and mussed his hair, but lovingly. "And tomorrow I will have mine, as it will be my turn."

And with that, we said good night.

ong ago, back when everyone had gone, we lived in a tower called the Morningside at the same time as this woman named Bezi Duras—she seemed old to me then, but as I'm now approaching what was probably her age myself, I'm beginning to think she wasn't.

The people for whom the tower was built had all left the city, and the new apartments sat empty until someone at the top figured having a few units occupied might give the looters pause. My late father had served the city with some loyalty and brains, so my mother and I were allowed to move in at a greatly reduced price. When we walked home from the bakery at night, the Morningside loomed before us with just a few thin, lighted windows skittering up the black edifice like notes of a secret song.

My mother and I lived on the 10th floor. Bezi Duras lived on the 14th. We knew this because we sometimes got caught in the elevator when she summoned it and had to ride up and then interminably back down with her, and her powerful tobacco smell, and the three huge, barrel-chested black dogs who towed her around the neighborhood at sundown.

Small and sharp-featured, Bezi was a source of fascination for all. She had come to the city after some faraway war whose particulars nobody, not even my mother, seemed to fully grasp. Nobody knew where she'd gotten such fine clothes, or what connection she had managed to press to get herself into the Morningside. She spoke to the dogs in a language nobody understood, and the police came around every so often to check whether the dogs had finally overpowered and eaten her, as they were said to have done to some poor bastard who tried to rob her on one of her walks. The incident was only a rumor, of course, but it was enough for the building to begin petitioning her to get rid of the dogs.

"Well, that'll never happen," my friend Arlo, who lived in the park with his macaw, told me.

"Why?"

"Because, honey, those dogs are her brothers."

I was never under the illusion that Arlo meant this in some metaphorical sense. In fact, he'd heard it from the macaw, who'd heard it from the dogs personally. They had been beautiful boys once, charming and accomplished; but somewhere in the course of Bezi's journey from her homeland to ours, life made it impossible for them to accompany her in their God-given forms. So according to Arlo, Bezi had struck a bargain with some entity, who turned them into dogs.

"Those dogs?" I asked, thinking of their foam-coated jowls and furrowed faces.

"They do make an impression. But I guess that's the point."

"But why?"

"Well, they're more welcome here than most people, honey."

I gave Arlo a hard time about a lot of things, but I believed him about the dogs—mostly because I was eight and felt his macaw incapable of telling a lie. Also, there was plenty of evidence to favor his theory. Those dogs ate better than we did. Every other afternoon, Bezi would come back from the butcher's laden with paper bags, and afterward the whole building smelled of roasted bones. She never spoke to the dogs in anything louder than a whisper, and they walked in a tight V around her when they left the building every night, never to be seen until the next morning, when she would come hurrying along the dawn-reddened street behind them as though only a matter of seconds stood between her and the total unraveling of her life. Her apartment, four floors above, had the same floor plan as our own, and it was easy to picture the dogs roaming around her cavernous place, following her with their yellow eyes, snoring on the white painter's tarp I always imagined covering the floor.

There were a lot of easily deducible things people missed about Bezi. That she was clearly a painter was the most significant one. Her ornate jackets and fine leather boots were always splashed with color. It darkened her nail beds, speckled her eyelashes, so bright that it was easily observable from the tree I sometimes watched her from at the end of the block, and in which the dogs occasionally sniffed me out, surrounding the trunk and roaring with frustration until Bezi's head finally appeared below, and she started in on me in that rickety language she had brought from home.

"You understand her, right?" I once asked my friend Ena, who had moved to New York from what I gathered was more or less the same place as Bezi.

"No," said Ena scornfully. "It's a completely different language."

"It sounds similar."

"Well, it's not."

Ena moved in with her aunt on the fourth floor only the previous year, after her family spent seven months at the quarantine depot, where Ena caught some illness—not the one for which she was being screened, mind you—and lost about half her body weight, so that when we walked down the street together, I felt obliged to tether her to me with one hand lest she blow away up the hill and into the river. She seemed unaware of her own smallness. She was grim and green-eyed, and had learned to pick locks in the camp (I always thought she meant camp as in summer camp; but she always called it the camp, which I eventually understood was different). Anyway, her lock-picking got us into parts of the Morningside that were previously inaccessible to me: the basement pool, for instance, with its dry mermaid mosaics; or the rooftop, which put us at eye level with the dark parapets of midtown.

Ena's curiosity made her a natural skeptic. She didn't buy into all that stuff about Bezi Duras's dog brothers turning into men from dawn till dusk—even when I laid out all the evidence and played *Swan Lake* for her.

"Who turned them?" she wanted to know.

"What?"

"Who turned them into dogs for her?"

"I don't know—aren't there people who do that kind of thing, where you come from?"

Ena grew red. "I'm telling you, Bezi Duras and I don't come from the same place."

All summer, this disagreement proved the sourest thing between us; impossible to reconcile, because it was dredged up every time Bezi set off down the street for the butcher's.

"What if we got into her place to see for ourselves?" Ena said one afternoon. "It wouldn't be hard."

"But crazy," I said, "since we know the place is guarded by a bunch of dogs."

Ena smirked. "If you're right, though, wouldn't they actually be men?"

"Wouldn't that be worse?" I had the sense that men in such a state would almost certainly be naked.

The possibility of breaking into Bezi's place would probably have continued to serve as a mere goad, had Bezi not paused where we were sitting on the park wall one bright afternoon and stared hard at Ena. "You're Neven's daughter, aren't you?" Bezi eventually said.

"That's right."

"Do you know what they used to call your father, back where I come from?"

Ena shrugged in a practiced way. Nothing could move her: not her dead father's name, and not whatever Bezi said next in that language I couldn't understand. She just sat there with her thin little legs pressed against the wall. "Sorry," she said when Bezi finally quieted. "I don't understand you."

I suppose I should've known this would seal Ena's decision to break into Bezi's place. But I was naive, and a little in love with her, and I had been there so often in my imaginary wanderings that it didn't seem all that remarkable when Ena pressed the up instead of down elevator button the following week. I believe I did say, "Let's not!"—only once, when Ena was already picking the lock, and only because I found myself sharply aware for the first time that we were, in fact, just kids.

The apartment was exactly the same as mine: still white hallways, a too-big kitchen with a marble countertop as thick as a cake. We followed the smell of paint into a parlor where a piano should have been. Leaning up against the wall there, surrounded on all sides by smaller canvases electric with color, stood the biggest painting I'd ever seen. The strokes were choppy and ragged, but the scene was easy enough to make out: a young woman was crossing a bridge from some little riverside town. Around her stood three empty spaces where the paint seemed to have been scrubbed away; presumably, I realized, this was where the dogs climbed out when they turned into their human form.

But they were not in their human form now. They were rousing themselves from a deep slumber where they lay sprawled out on that sure-enough paint-splattered tarp, sitting up one by one, as surprised, I think, to see us as we were to see them.

What would have happened had Bezi not come back at that exact moment, I really can't say. We probably would've ended up as one of those tragic statistics you read about in the paper that teach you what kind of being is safe and what kind is not.

"Well," Bezi said. "Neven's daughter. Twisted at heart—what a surprise."

"Go to hell," Ena said through her tears.

My mother never found out, and I guess Ena's didn't either. For years, that moment, known only to the three of us, was the first thing I thought about when I woke, and the last thing I thought about as I lay in the dark. I was certain I would revisit it every day of my life. And for a long time, even after we left the Morningside, I did. And then time passed, and eventually I did not. It would suddenly occur to me that a few days had gone by without my thinking about it—which, of course, would break my streak, and I'd feel relieved to find myself suddenly plunged back into that room, with its huge painting, and the dogs around it as though they were waiting to be called back into the world from which they had come. But then that got hazy, too. It became the kind of thing I'd tell lovers after deciding they would probably be sticking around. The kind of thing I hoped they'd forget about me when we parted ways.

By the time I stumbled on this story in the paper, I

hadn't thought about it in years. A foreign painter of some celebrity died in the city last summer; the problem was, her body couldn't be retrieved because it was guarded by a pack of starving Rottweilers, who would go wild if anyone so much as touched the door. Experts from all over the coast were brought in, but no one could find a command to subdue the dogs. It was decided that they should be shot, and a brave sniper was hoisted up on a window-washing rig for that purpose. But when he peered inside, he saw only the lifeless old woman, lying with her hands crossed on a tarp at the foot of an enormous painting of a princess and three young men. What exactly was he supposed to shoot? "It's baffling," he told the reporter, "but there's really nothing for me to do here." After he packed up, the police tried the door again; and sure enough the dogs came roaring back.

Finally, after about a week of this, a woman who worked across town showed up at the police station. "I used to live there," she said. "I can help." The reporter didn't name her but described her as rail-thin, with huge green eyes, so I know it was Ena who went up there one wild evening with what was left of the city gathered in the courtyard below; Ena who stood outside the door, whispering endearments of some bygone age, of some place that no longer existed, in that language she'd always known the dogs would understand, until she heard them move back from the door, and she turned the knob, saying, don't worry, boys, it's all right, it's all right, it's all right.

SCREEN·TIME
BY ALEJANDRO ZAMBRA

Translated by Megan McDowell from the Spanish

any times over his two years of life, the boy has heard laughter or cries coming from his parents' bedroom. It's hard to know how he would react if he ever found out what his parents really do while he's asleep: watch TV.

He's never watched TV or anyone watching TV, so his parents' television is vaguely mysterious to him: Its screen is a sort of mirror, but the image it reflects is opaque, insufficient, and you can't draw on it in the steam, though sometimes a layer of dust allows for similar games.

Still, the boy wouldn't be surprised to learn that this screen reproduces images in movement. He is occasionally allowed to see other people on screens, most often people in his second country. Because the boy has two countries: his mother's, which is his main country, and his father's, which is his secondary country. His father doesn't live there, but his father's parents do, and they're the people the boy sees most often on-screen.

He has also seen his grandparents in person, because the

boy has traveled twice to his second country. He doesn't remember the first trip, but by the second he could walk on his own and talk himself blue in the face, and those weeks were unforgettable, though the most memorable event happened on the flight there, when a screen that seemed every bit as useless as his parents' TV lit up, and suddenly there was a friendly red monster who referred to himself in the third person. The monster and the boy were immediate friends, perhaps because back then the boy also talked about himself in the third person.

The meeting was fortuitous, really, because the boy's parents didn't plan to watch TV during the trip. The flight began with a couple of naps, and then his parents opened the little suitcase that held seven books and five zoomorphic puppets, and a long time was spent on the reading and immediate rereading of those books, punctuated by insolent comments from the puppets, who also gave their opinions on the shapes of the clouds and the quality of the snacks. Everything was going swimmingly until the boy asked for a toy that had chosen to travel—his parents explained—in the hold of the plane, and then he remembered several others that—who knows why—had decided to stay in his main country. Then, for the first time in six hours, the boy burst into tears that lasted a full minute, which isn't a long time, but, to a man in the seat behind them, seemed very long indeed.

"Make that kid shut up!" bellowed the man.

The boy's mother turned around and looked at him

with serene contempt, and, after a well-executed pause, she lowered her gaze to stare fixedly between his legs and said, without the slightest trace of aggression:

"Must be really tiny."

The man apparently had no defense against such an accusation and didn't reply. The boy—who had stopped crying by then—moved to his mother's arms, and then it was the father's turn. He also knelt in his seat to stare at the man; he didn't insult him, but merely asked his name.

"Enrique Elizalde," said the man, with the little dignity he had left.

"Thanks."

"Why do you want to know?"

"I have my reasons."

"Who are you?"

"I don't want to tell you, but you'll find out. Soon you'll know full well who I am."

The father glared several more seconds at the now-remorseful or desperate Enrique Elizalde, and he would have kept it up except that a bout of turbulence forced him to refasten his seat belt.

"This jerk thinks I'm really powerful," he murmured then, in English, which was the language the parents used instinctively now to insult other people.

"We should at least name a character after him," said the mother.

"Good idea! I'll name all the bad guys in my books Enrique Elizalde."

"Me too! I guess we'll have to start writing books with bad guys," she said.

And that was when they turned on the screen in front of them and tuned in to the show of the happy, hairy red monster. The show lasted 20 minutes, and when the screen went dark, the boy protested, but his parents explained that the monster's presence wasn't repeatable, he wasn't like books, which could be read over and over.

During the three weeks they were in his secondary country, the boy asked about the monster daily, and his parents explained that he only lived on airplanes. The re-encounter finally came on the flight home, and it lasted another scant 20 minutes. Two months after their return, since the boy still spoke of the monster with a certain melancholy, his parents bought him a stuffed replica, which the boy saw as the authentic original. Since then the two have been inseparable: In fact, right now, the boy has just fallen asleep hugging the red plush toy, while his parents have retired to the bedroom, and surely they will soon turn on the TV. There's a chance, if things go as they usually do, that this story will end with the two of them watching TV.

The boy's father grew up with the TV always on, and at his son's age he was possibly unaware that the television could even be turned off. The boy's mother, on the other hand, had been kept away from TV for an astonishing 10 years. Her own mother's official version was that the TV signal didn't reach as far as their house on the outskirts of the city, so that the TV seemed to the girl a completely useless object. One day she invited a classmate over to play, and without asking anyone the friend simply plugged in the TV and turned it on. There was no disillusionment or crisis: The girl thought the TV signal had only just reached the city's periphery. She ran to relay the good news to her mother, who, though she was an atheist, fell to her knees, raised her arms to the sky, and shouted histrionically, persuasively, "It's a MIRACLE!"

In spite of these very different backgrounds, the couple are in complete agreement that it's best to put off their son's exposure to screens as long as possible. They're not fanatics, in any case, they're not against TV by any means. When they first met, they often employed the hackneyed strategy of meeting up to watch movies as a pretext for sex. Later, in the period that could be considered the boy's prehistory, they succumbed to the spell of many excellent series. And they never watched as much TV as during the months leading up to the birth of their son, whose intrauterine life was set not to Mozart symphonies or lullabies but rather to the theme songs of series about bloody power struggles in an unspecified ancient time of zombies and dragons, or in the spacious government house of the self-designated "leader of the free world."

When the boy was born, the couple's TV experience changed radically. At the end of the day their physical and mental exhaustion allowed only 30 or 40 minutes of waning concentration, so that almost without realizing it they lowered their standards and became habitual viewers of mediocre series. They still wanted to immerse themselves in unfathomable realms and live vicariously through challenging and complex experiences that forced them to seriously rethink their place in the world, but that's what the books they read during the day were for; at night they wanted easy laughter, funny dialogue, and scripts that granted the sad satisfaction of understanding without the slightest effort.

Someday, maybe in one or two years, they plan to spend Saturday or Sunday afternoons watching movies with the boy, and they even keep a list of the ones they want to watch as a family. But for now, the TV is relegated to that final hour of the day when the boy is asleep and the mother and father return, momentarily, to being simply she and he—she, in bed looking at her phone, and he, lying faceup on the floor as if resting after a round of sit-ups. Suddenly he gets up and lies on the bed, too, and his hand reaches for the remote but changes course, picks up the nail clippers instead, and he starts to cut his fingernails. She looks at him and thinks that lately, he is always clipping his nails.

"We're going to be shut in for months. He's going to get bored," she says.

"They'll let people walk their dogs, but not their kids," he says bitterly.

"I'm sure he doesn't like this. Maybe he doesn't show it, but he must be having a horrible time. How much do you think he understands?"

"About as much as we do."

"And what do we understand?" she asks, in the tone of a student reviewing a lesson before a test. It's almost as if she had asked, "What is photosynthesis?"

"That we can't go out because there's a shitty virus. That's all."

"That what used to be allowed is now forbidden. And what used to be forbidden still is."

"He misses the park, the bookstore, museums. Same as we do."

"The zoo," she says. "He doesn't talk about it, but he complains more, gets mad more often. Not much, but more."

"But he doesn't miss preschool, not at all," he says.

"I hope it's just two or three months. What if it's more? A whole year?"

"I don't think so," he says. He'd like to sound more convinced.

"What if this is our world from now on? What if after this virus there's another and another?" She asks the question but it could just as well be him, with the same words and the same anxious intonation.

During the day they take turns: One of them watches their son while the other works. They are behind on everything, and although everyone is behind on everything, they feel sure that they're a little more behind than everyone else. They should argue, compete over which of them has the more urgent and better-paid job, but instead they both offer to watch the boy full-time, because that half-day with him is an interval of true happiness, genuine laughter, purifying evasion—they would rather spend the whole day playing ball in the hallway or drawing unintentionally monstrous creatures on the small square of wall where drawing is allowed or strumming guitar while the boy turns the pegs until it's out of tune or reading stories that they now find perfect, much better than the books they themselves write, or try to. Even if they only had one of those children's stories, they would rather read it nonstop all day than sit in front of their computers, the awful news radio on in the background, to send reply emails full of apologies for the delay and to stare at the stupid map of real-time contagion and death—he looks, especially, at his son's secondary country, which of course is still his primary one, and he thinks of his parents and imagines that in the hours or days since he last talked to them they've gotten sick and he'll never see them again, and then he calls them and those calls leave him shattered, but he doesn't say anything, at least not to her, because she has spent weeks now in a slow and imperfect anxiety that makes her think she should learn to embroider, or at least stop reading the beautiful and hopeless novels she reads, and she also thinks that she should have become something other than a writer; they agree on that, they've talked about it many times, because so often—every time they try to write— they've felt the inescapable futility of each and every word.

"Let's let him watch movies," she says. "Why not? Only on Sundays."

"At least then we'd know if it's Monday or Thursday or Sunday," he says.

"What's today?"

"I think it's Tuesday."

"Let's decide tomorrow," she says.

He finishes cutting his nails and looks at his hands with uncertain satisfaction, or maybe as if he had just finished cutting someone else's nails, or as if he were looking at the nails of a person who just cut their own nails and was asking him, for some reason (maybe because he's become an expert), for his opinion or approval.

"They're growing faster," he says.

"Didn't you just cut them last night?"

"Exactly, they're growing faster." He says this very seriously. "Every night it seems like they've grown out during the day. Abnormally fast."

"I think it's good for nails to grow fast. Supposedly they grow faster at the beach," she says, sounding as if she's trying to remember something, maybe the feeling of waking up on the beach with the sun in her face.

"I think mine are a record."

"Mine are growing faster, too," she says, smiling. "Even faster than yours. By noon they're practically claws. And I cut them and they grow again."

"I'm pretty sure mine grow faster than yours."

"No way."

Then they put their hands together as if they could really see their fingernails growing, as if they could compare speeds, and what should be a quick scene lengthens out, because they let themselves get caught up in the absurd illusion of that silent competition, beautiful and useless, which lasts so long that even the most patient viewer would turn off the TV in indignation. But no one is watching them, though the TV screen is like a camera that records their bodies frozen in that strange and funny pose. A monitor amplifies the boy's breathing, and it's the only sound that accompanies the contest of their hands, their nails, a contest that lasts several minutes but not long enough for anyone to win, and that ends, finally, with the longed-for burst of warm, frank laughter that they were really needing.

HOW WE USED TO PLAY
BY DINAW MENGESTU

efore the virus hit, my uncle drove his cab 10 to 12 hours a day, six days a week, for nearly two decades. He continued doing so even though every month he had fewer and fewer customers and sometimes spent hours idling outside one of the luxury hotels near the Capitol Building waiting for a fare. He was still living in the same apartment he moved into when he first arrived in America, in 1978, and when I called to ask him how he was doing, he told me, more amused than alarmed, that until now, he had failed to consider the possibility that he might someday die in that building. "Why don't they tell you this when you sign the lease? If you are over seventy, it should be right there, at the very top. Be careful. This may be the last place you ever live."

I assured him there was no chance of him dying, even though we both knew that wasn't true. He was 72, and every morning before getting into his cab, he walked up and down the 12 stories of his apartment building to warm up his muscles before work.

"You're the strongest man I know," I told him. "It would take an alien virus to knock you out."

Before getting off the phone I told him I was going to drive down from New York to see him. It was March 12, 2020, and the virus was about to lay siege to the city. "We'll go to the grocery store," I said. "And stuff your freezer so you can grow old and fat until the virus disappears." I left New York early the next morning to find the highways between New York and DC already crowded with SUVs. On his only visit to New York, my uncle asked me what happened to all the cars buried deep underground in expensive parking lots scattered throughout the city. Before buying his own cab, he had worked for 15 years in a parking garage three blocks from the White House, and he often said that he would never understand why Americans spent so much money to park big cars they never drove. As I passed my first hour in traffic, I thought of calling to tell him I finally had the answer to his question. For all the talk of American optimism, we were obsessed with apocalypse, and those big empty cars that now filled all four lanes of the highway had simply been waiting for the right explosion to hit the road.

When I finally reached my uncle's apartment, in a suburb just outside DC, he was sitting on one of the concrete benches in front of his building, his palms pressed together with both elbows on his knees. He motioned with his hands for me to stay where I was and got into his cab, which was parked a few feet behind me. He sent me a text message: "Park. I am driving."

We greeted each other awkwardly, a triple tap of shoulders rather than the customary kiss on the cheek. It had been six, maybe seven months since we had seen each other, and at least a decade since I had been in his cab. As we pulled away from his building, he said this trip reminded him of a game we used to play when I was a child and he would drive my mother and me to the grocery.

"Do you remember that?" he asked me. "Do you remember how we used to play?"

We turned right onto a wide four-lane road lined with shopping malls and car dealerships, none of which were there when I was growing up. For some reason, it seemed too much to respond to my uncle's question with a simple answer like, Of course I remember those games; they were often my favorite part of the week. So instead I nodded and complained about the traffic building ahead of us. My uncle rubbed his hand affectionately across the back of my head and then turned the meter on. That was how the games we had played in his cab always began, with a flip of the meter and him turning toward the back seat to ask me, "Where would you like to go, sir?" Over the few months we played that game, we never repeated the same place twice. We started local—the Washington Monument, the museums along the Mall—but then quickly expanded to increasingly remote destinations: the Pacific Ocean, Disney World and Disneyland, Mount Rushmore and Yellowstone National Park, and then once I learned more about world history and geography, Egypt and the Great Wall of China, followed by Big Ben and the Colosseum in Rome.

"Your mother used to get mad at me for not telling you to choose Ethiopia," he said. "She used to tell me, 'If he is going to imagine something, let him imagine his home country.' I tried to tell her you were a child. You were born in America. You didn't have a country. The only thing you were loyal to was us."

The light ahead of us turned red and then green three times before we finally moved forward, a pace that would have normally infuriated my uncle, who by his own admission had never been good at staying still. The last time we played that game my uncle argued with my mother about the futility of our fictional adventures. "We can't afford to take him anywhere," he said. "So let him see the world from the back seat of a taxi."

The final trip we took was to Australia, and my mother let us take it on the condition that we never again played the game with her in the car. Once we agreed to her terms, my uncle turned the meter on, and for the next 15 minutes I told him everything I knew about the landscape and wildlife of Australia. I continued talking even after we arrived at the grocery store and my mother told me to get out of the car. I wasn't prepared to see my trip end in a parking lot, and so my uncle waved my mother away and told me to keep talking. "Tell me everything you know about Australia," he said, just as a deep tiredness came over me. I took my shoes off and stretched my legs out. I folded my legs underneath me as he placed a thick road map from the glove compartment under my head so my face wouldn't stick to the vinyl seats.

"Sleep," he told me. "Australia is very far away. You must be tired from the jet lag."

I thought of asking my uncle what, if anything, he remembered of our final trip as we neared the grocery store. He was focused on trying to turn right into a parking lot already crowded with cars and what looked to be a half-dozen police cars angled around the entrance. We only had a few hundred feet left, but given the line of cars and the growing crowd waiting outside, carts in hand, it seemed increasingly unlikely that we would make it inside before the shelves were picked bare.

It must have taken us close to 20 minutes to make that final turn into the parking lot, a minor victory that my uncle acknowledged by tapping the meter twice with his index finger so I could take note of the fare.

"Finally," he said. "After all these years in America, I'm rich."

We inched our way toward the rear of the lot, where it seemed more likely we would find a place to park. When that failed, my uncle drove over a strip of grass into an adjacent restaurant lot that had customer-only parking signs pinned to the wall. I waited for him to turn off the engine, but he kept both hands on the steering wheel, his body pitched slightly forward as if he were preparing to drive away again but wasn't sure which direction to turn toward. I thought briefly that I understood what was troubling him.

"You don't have to go into the store," I said. "You can wait here and pick me up when I come out."

141

He turned to face me then. It was the first time we had looked directly at each other since I entered the cab.

"I don't want to wait in a parking lot," he said. "I do that every day."

"Then what do you want?"

He switched the meter off, and then the engine, but left the key in the ignition.

"I want to go back home," he said. "I want someone to tell me how to get out of here."

LINE 19 WOODSTOCK/GLISAN
BY KAREN RUSSELL

t happened just like people said: Time really did slow down. The ambulance came screaming toward the Line 19 bus, crossing the Burnside Bridge in the wrong lane. Scan right, scan left, scan again—Valerie was mindful of her bus's many blind spots. But the ambulance had appeared out of nowhere, birthed from the thickest fog she'd ever seen. Larger, closer, slower and slower, it advanced. Time pulled away like black taffy. Even the sirens seemed to groggily blink. It took Valerie half a century to turn the wheel, and by then it was too late: They were stuck.

Valerie was an excellent driver. In 14 years she had only two SIPs on her record, both utter bullshit. Her mother, Tamara, 72 and recovering from a stroke, was home with Val's 15-year-old son, Teak. Teak collected novelty bongs; Nana hoarded Reese's Peanut Butter Cups. Her mother had been coughing for the past week. Keep her home until she gets a fever, the doctor had told her. Until? "Take Nana's temperature," she whispered to Teak before leaving. And to her mother, top volume: "His gummies aren't 'vitamins,' Ma."

Her bus was less than a third full on the night of the accident. Weekly ridership was down 63 percent since February.

145

Teenagers still boarded, cavalier and horny, treating the city bus as their Ass-Express—Teak's explanation. (He'd sounded a little jealous, she thought. Teak was a loner, like her.) Valerie had been keeping her eye on two baby-faced girls in the back who had lowered their masks to make out. They didn't have a death wish; they had a life wish so extreme it led them to the same end. You couldn't convince these kids that they were vulnerable to any threat worse than a fatal loneliness.

"Hey, Juliets." Val's voice sounded husky behind her mask. "Knock it off."

"I'm her contact tracer," the blue-haired one called back, licking her honey's neck. Valerie did not join in their laughter. "As long as you're not licking my poles. . . ."

Valerie called her lunar-hour regulars "the Last Bus Club." On any given weeknight, she'd have eight or ten familiar faces. Covid had shifted the Last Bus Club's demographics—now a majority of her riders were people for whom "state of emergency" was a chronic condition. Riders like Marla, who had no car and needed medicine, tampons, food. Marla had wheeled up the ramp at the Chávez stop, a soaking Rite Aid bag on her lap. "You're it," Valerie had said, kneeling to secure Marla's chair. "New rules. Can't have a packed bus."

Silver lining, Val worried less about vehicular manslaughter. The virus had cleared the streets. Many fewer pedestrians zombie-waddling around, stepping blindly off curbs. Sis! Pull the plugs out of your ears! Bicyclists: Is it wise to dress like mimes?

Some of her colleagues called the riders "cattle," but she'd never gone in for that. Did she love her riders? The way some of the older drivers claimed to love their regulars? "I love these benefits," she said to Freddie. She worked this job because it was the highest hourly wage she could make for Teak. "You're saving for retirement? I'm saving for my embolism," she joked.

"How many good people do you think there are in the world?" Freddie had asked her in the break room. She'd answered without hesitation: "Twenty percent of them. Some nights, eleven."

Piss bus. Fire in the shelter. Loud and Verbal. Loose dog on Rex and 32nd. Pass up throwing rocks. Weather. Possible Covid rider. Even before the accident that stopped Time, it had been quite a week.

Lots of sharks swimming alongside the fish in this life. Some of her regulars, she did care about—gentle men like Ben who just wanted to get out of the freezing rain, Marla in her spray-painted wheelchair, knitting webby red yarn "dragon wings" for her grandson. No cash fare at the moment, and these nights she didn't bother pressing people if they didn't have a Hop card.

At the station, she got a Ziploc bag with a single paper mask and eight Clorox wipes. She bought her own bleach, misted everything down. Freddie had hung up a Dollar Tree shower curtain to protect himself, before the bosses ordered him to remove it.

Earlier that night, Val missed an omen. It happened

rolling toward Powell: dozens of shuttered bars and vintage shops, each one like an eccentric aunt, shaggy bungalows, derelict rosebushes, backstops and hoops. She almost screamed when she swerved around a kid's bicycle lying in the road. Her headlights shined on its twisted form. Ribbons spilling around the handlebars, training wheels with finger-bone spokes. Her heart was going nine cups of coffee. Nobody there. Nobody hurt. The bus roared on. Cupped in the side mirror, the bicycle became a dull speck, shrinking away like childhood itself. Her pulse fell, and she merged back into her ordinary concerns.

A good driver's biography is a thousand pages of non-events and near misses. Valerie counted these shadows as blessings.

But now, it seemed, her luck had run out. Dimly she was aware of her riders screaming behind her. Valerie braced for a collision that did not happen. What the hell was going on? The ambulance driver, it appeared, was mouthing the same question, with more profanities. It was as if they were stuck in some kind of invisible putty. Two frightened young faces crept into focus, sharpening like film in a developing tray. The bus rolled forward another inch before it stopped with an otherworldly shrieking, a breath away from the ambulance's grille. Valerie waited for a wave of relief that never came. Needlessly, she applied the emergency brake. The clock had frozen at 8:48 p.m. She jumped down.

"Valerie."

"Yvonne."

"Danny."

They shook hands solemnly on the bridge.

"There was nobody on the road tonight," said Danny, the driver. He had lacquered black fingernails, a starched EMS shirt. His white face looked greenish in her headlights. "I didn't realize I was in the wrong lane. So much fog and my defroster is terrible. . . ."

Out of the corner of her eye, she was aware of what she wasn't seeing: firefly headlights racing down Naito, the wide river spinning its geometries toward the Pacific. Nothing around them moved. Darkness lidded the bridge.

"I just want to get back on the road," Valerie said. She couldn't afford another SIP. They went on your record permanently, and if you complained about unfairness, it was another strike against you.

"Oh, my goodness," said Yvonne, the paramedic riding shotgun. A Black woman with clear-rimmed glasses and wide, amber eyes, maybe a few years older than Teak. It surprised Valerie, how self-conscious these young people made her feel about her grays. Also that it was still possible to feel vain about your hair, when you were facing down eternity.

"I apologize. I didn't mean to shake hands."

Valerie nodded, grateful for her mask. She'd forgotten, too. She was terrified of giving the virus to her mother. Nana had a pelican smile now, her right side paralyzed. She worried that it made her look mean, but Teak reassured his grandma that she'd looked mean as hell before the stroke. Only he could make the smile reach her eyes.

"It was the scariest thing," Yvonne said. "You were coming at us slower and slower—"

"I was coming at you?"

"And then everything just . . . stopped—"

They all stared at the quiet ambulance, then turned together to the bus. Valerie's riders were making large gestures behind the arched eyebrows of the windshield wipers. They looked rattled, but unhurt.

Something very strange had happened to the outer world. The Willamette River had stopped flowing; it looked icy and sculptural beyond the railings. Bars of light appeared and vanished on the bridge trestles, the deep water. Purple, maroon, palest green. As if the moon were dealing out cards, randomly laying down colors.

Valerie climbed back into the bus cab. She called in to the dispatcher: "1902. I had an accident on the Burnside Bridge. I think I'm stuck between worlds. Or possibly dead."

The dispatcher could no longer, it seemed, hear her. "1902 here, on the bridge, do you copy?"

"Help me," she whispered.

She hadn't really expected an answer. What surprised her was the speed with which her confusion turned into horror, her horror into a stupefied resignation. The 19 was lost in Time.

Valerie did not consider herself a graceful person. She had flat feet and asthma. She drove a 40-foot, 20-ton bus. And yet her mind did a gymnastic leap to the worst-case scenario: I might never get home to them.

She gulped back a flavor of terror that was entirely new to her. Could things end this way, the bus simply sliding off the table and into a cul-de-sac of space-time, like a cue ball sinking into the wrong pocket?

People were texting frantically, thumbing hysterical monologues into their phones.

She felt a stab of nostalgia for the anxieties of 8:47 p.m. Loud and Verbal was a problem she understood.

"Silent Night," she murmured into the dead receiver.

Swallowed Panic. Quiet Hiss.

"Everybody off!"

Valerie and Yvonne decided to walk for help. Without turning, Valerie could feel the others following them. When they reached the ambulance, Valerie felt as if she were walking into a gale. Doubled over, she pushed until she could advance no farther. Valerie turned to see half her riders struggling in the opposite direction, taking tai chi steps through a thickening mist. They looked like trees, slowly lifting their roots and then replanting them.

"You sound high, Mom!" Teak would say, if she ever saw Teak again.

With a cry, she ran at the secret wall, catapulting her fists at the air. She made it 10 feet beyond the ambulance. Her legs fought a crushing pressure, her arms flattening to her sides.

"Should we really call it 'the accident'?" Danny was asking, a little defensively. "Nothing happened—" He gestured at the ambulance, with its uncrumpled hood and its unshattered windshield, its undeployed airbags and its unbloodied seats.

"Are you joking? Time stopped moving!" she said.

One of her regulars, Humberto, "Bertie" on his name tag, had an old-fashioned watch, and he showed her that the minute hand had stopped, its tiny gears frozen. "It's fake," he said, embarrassed and agitated. "I mean, it tells time, but it's not real gold." He shook it angrily, and then with a cry chucked it over the railing. A nearly 80-foot fall. The night swallowed it whole, and Valerie wondered if it ever reached the water.

"Hey, watch out! Six feet, buddy!"

"Oh, sorry." Even this close to midnight, you could hear people blushing.

Ben, who suffered from paranoid delusions, seemed curiously sanguine. "Look, I have some spicy chicken here. So we won't starve." He unlidded a bucket, offered it around. There was nothing in it.

"We're dead, we're dead," the young mother in the goldenrod hijab said, and she began to cry.

This was Fatima, a labor-and-delivery nurse and three-year member of the Last Bus Club. She worked nights at the hospital. Her son was in his grandmother's arms in Montavilla, on the other side of the black river, waiting to be picked up.

"Oh, I need to get to my baby—"

"Everybody has somewhere to be, lady. You're not special."

"Not everybody," Ben said softly.

Valerie revised the sentence for Fatima.

"He's right. You're not alone. My boy is waiting on me, too."

And now they let the ghosts out of their bodies, sighing. Beautiful phantoms, calling to them from either end of the bridge.

"My fiancée is pregnant. . . ."

"My sick brother. . . ."

"I need to feed Genevieve, my caiman. . . ."

Danny cleared his throat. "I know it's not a competition. I'm not trying to one-up anybody here. But we were dispatched to help a woman having a seizure in a hot tub. . . ."

This was not well received by Valerie's passengers: "Well, you should have thought about that before you tried to run us off the road!"

"Pick a lane, son."

"Preferably not our lane, next time."

"If you're all such great drivers," Danny exploded, "why are you riding *the bus*?"

It was nice to hear them complaining, actually. It was a song Valerie knew by heart, the ballad of the disappointed rider. Her bus had broken down many, many times. Two flats on Flavel, in Vesuvian July. Electrical problems across the street from Pioneer Square. Nobody ever said, Oh, that's OK, Val, I don't mind waiting an extra hour to get where I'm going.

This was an unprecedented crisis. But here, at last, was

a familiar feeling. No reinforcements were coming to help them. The nine of them would have to muscle up some solution, Valerie announced.

Now the mood among the Last Bus Club shifted. Everybody wanted to help, a desire that surged and splintered into a hundred tiny actions. Humberto looked under the hood. The blue-haired girl slid between the rear tires, sleuthing for clues. Yvonne and Danny tried to jump-start the ambulance clock. Was it the weight of these small efforts that began to multiply, refreighting the moment, unsticking it from the cosmic mud? Or was it Fatima's birth plan?

"Listen. I don't know why I didn't think of this before. We are stuck in the canyon between 8:48 and 8:49. This happens during birth, sometimes. And fear shuts everything down."

The bus seemed to be patiently waiting to be smashed into the railing.

Fatima explained how she turned breech babies around. She wanted them to try her techniques on the 19. "Danny, I want you to stand at the back of the bus. Humberto, don't strain your neck like that, let me reposition you. . . ."

Fatima insisted on safety. They spaced themselves out, up and down the bus. The important thing, Fatima said, was to sing. An old trick, she explained, for speeding up a birth. "It opens up the mouth, the throat . . . everything." She drew an S in the air, pointing from her lips up to the stars. "Something is jammed. I don't understand why this happened. But I know how to restart a stalled labor."

What else could they do? The Last Bus Club followed her instructions. They chanted with her. Two shallow breaths, one exhalation from the diaphragm. They sang, the wordless song of animals, a mounting pressure you could feel in the charged and slippery air. The bridge began to subtly vibrate; a few bars of the song later, to moan. People's lungs and arms were on fire, but the bus would not budge. Danny and Humberto and Ben and Marla and Yvonne and Valerie and Fatima and the Juliets exhaled as one, heaving against it. Fatima smiled and pointed. Almost imperceptibly, the tires began to roll.

Push! Push!

A shower of sparks. Little orange mohawks of fire on the blue treads.

Fatima turned to Danny and Yvonne:

"Why don't you two get back into the ambulance?"

"I don't want to die!" Danny screamed.

"Put the vehicle in reverse," Fatima said gently.

She and Yvonne exchanged a glance. "Long night," Yvonne mouthed.

Later, there would be plenty of time for disagreement; half of them would maintain that Time would have simply thawed on its own; their actions had nothing to do with it. Others felt certain that a muscular, united effort had saved them. Although which muscles had done it? The singing, or the pushing?

"Everybody back in your seats! Just as you were!" It was Marla, an orchid lover, who made the suggestion. "Estivation" was a word for petals and sepals arranged in tight symmetry inside a bud. They would channel the energy of a flower pushing through soil. The Last Bus Club sang together in the back of the bus, as if this were a school field trip at a Dantean rest stop. Valerie tipped her head back and howled. At last, the master key caused the engine to roar to life.

And then the tires squealed and rolled, a stomach-churning acceleration. The fog parted, revealing moving water. A hawk crossed the sky. A star fell. The ambulance reversed and sped off toward the next emergency. Newborn shadows congealed on the river. One of these began to swim, a little sluggishly, after the 19. Onboard, the teenage lovers were still singing, elated, very off-key. Minnows passing under the bridge crossed the flattened hulk of the reflected bus.

Valerie sped down Burnside under a moon that flashed like cellophane. The clock clicked over to 8:49. Omens hide in the weave of a day, a life, waiting to be recollected. Val remembered the tiny bicycle. Somewhere, a child was sleeping, red blood circulating in her body and nowhere near the road.

It felt almost like a numb foot coming awake.

As she drove, constellations of moments began to kaleidoscope through Val's body, painful and sharp—her mother lying on the floor, the white knife of Teak's birth, Freddie laughing tears over scalding coffee, the smell of smoldering rubber, her years coiling like circuitry. Now she could see by the real lights of her city: the haloed lobbies of the condominiums, the skeletal boats in the harbor. Tent camps and vacant hotels, butterflied around the river. The world they'd left was the one they returned to: trembling, rain-wet, lush, trashed, alive.

On the other side of the bridge, would they all stay in touch? Send one another holiday cards? Form a text group? Not likely. Already, Valerie could sense them segregating again. Hourly and salary. Southeast and Northwest. People with jobs and homes and destinations, and people like Ben. Some would forget as soon as they crossed the river, while others would be permanently haunted. And yet they'd shared a nightmare. A miraculous escape. Valerie braked, waiting on the light. She'd see Ben on her route tomorrow, on his endless carousel ride from Gateway to Mount Scott. Maybe they could talk about it, from behind their masks. The light turned green. Already, she was beginning to doubt it.

IF WISHES * WAS HORSES
BY DAVID MITCHELL

o sea view? For nine hundred quid a week? Trip-Advisor's gonna hear 'bout this."

She snorts. "On the plus side, Your Majesty, you've got your penthouse all to yourself. Jacuzzi. Sauna. Minibar." She taps in the code, swipes her card, and the LED goes green. "Home away from home." Bolts clunk and the door opens. Bog-standard 8-by-14-foot cell. Shitter. Desk. Chair. Locker. Dirty windows. Seen better. Seen worse.

The door shuts behind me—revealing the bunk bed with some bastard lying on the top. He's an Arab, Indian, Asian, something. He's as not pleased to see me as I'm not pleased to see him. I bang on the door. "Oy! Guard! This cell's occupied!"

No joy.

"Guard!"

Daft bloody moo's moved on.

Today's outlook: heavy cloud, all day.

Dump my bag on my bed. "Great." I look at the Asian bloke. He ain't got that Rottweiler glint, but yer don't take nothing for granted. I'm guessing he's Muslim. "Just came

161

from Wandsworth," I tell him. "I'm s'posed to be in quarantine. One to a cell. My cellmate had the virus."

"I tested positive," Asian Bloke says, "at Belmarsh."

Belmarsh is a Cat A prison. I'm thinking, Terrorism?

"No," Asian Bloke says. "I'm not an ISIS sympathizer. No, I don't pray toward Mecca. No, I don't have four wives and ten kids."

Can't deny I was thinking it. "Yer don't look ill."

"I'm asymptomatic." He clocks. I ain't sure what that means. "I've got the antibodies, so I don't get sick, but I have the virus, and I can pass it on. You really shouldn't have been put in here."

Voilà. Classic Ministry of Justice fuck-up. There's an emergency call button, so I press the CALL button.

"I was told the guards here cut the wires," Asian Bloke says. "Anything for a quiet life."

I believe it. "Prob'ly too late by now, anyway. Virus-wise."

He lights up a roll-up. "You may be right."

"Happy fucking birthday to me."

Water chunders down a pipe.

"Is it your birthday?" he asks.

"Just an expression."

Day 2. Pogo Hoggins, who I was banged up with at Wandsworth, snored like a Harrier jump jet. Zam the Asian Bloke's a silent sleeper, and I wake in OK nick. When the floor-hatch is slid open for the breakfast tray, I'm ready on my knees to get the porter's attention. "Oy, mate."

A weary-as-hell, "What?"

"First off, there's two of us banged up in here."

I see a Nike trainer, a shin, and a trolley wheel. "Not according to my printout." Big Black Geezer, by the sound of it.

Zam joins me at the gap. "Your printout's wrong, as you can hear. And we're supposed to be in isolation, in single cells."

Big Black Geezer shuts the hatch with his foot. It sticks for long enough for me to ask for a second breakfast box.

"Yeah, nice try." The hatch slams shut.

"You eat it," Zam says. "I'm not hungry."

The box has a pig on it, with a speech bubble saying, "Two succulent pork sausages!" "What, 'cause yer can't eat pork?"

"I eat very little. It's one of my superpowers."

So I wolf down the single sausage. It ain't succulent, and it ain't pork. I offer Zam the crackers and out-of-date yogurt. Once again, he says no. Don't need to be told twice.

Today's outlook: cloudy, with bright patches.

The telly's a knackered box of junk, but today it gives a bit o' Channel 5. *The Ricki Pickett Show.* Must be a repeat: Everyone's packed into the studio, breathing in one another's germs. Today's show's called *My Mum Cradle-Snatched My Boyfriend.* Used to watch Ricki Pickett with Kylie when she was pregnant with Gem. Used to find all them snarling whinging sad sacks tearing chunks out of each other funny. Not now. Even the saddest, poorest, and sorriest have got what I ain't. They don't even know it.

• • •

Day 3. Feel rough. Nasty cough. I asked Big Black Geezer for the doctor. Said he'd put me on the list, but he still gave us only one breakfast and one lunch box. Zam told me to eat it. Said I'd need to keep my strength up. Ain't been out of our cell once. No exercise yard. No shower. Thought quarantine'd be a doss, but it's bad as solitary. The telly gave us half an hour of ITV news. Prime Minister Spaffer Bumblefuck says, "Stay alert!" President Very Stable Genius says, "Drink bleach!" Half of America still reckons he's God's Gift. What a place. There was a bit about how the stars are coping with lockdown. Didn't know whether to laugh or cry. Then the telly conked out. Did a few press-ups, but my cough came back. Ain't only air I'm gasping for. I'll ask Big Black Geezer to hook me up with spice. Double bubble on tic but needs must. Lunch was powdered oxtail soup. Foxtail soup, more like. Drank it down and saw this rat on the edge of the sink. Big brown bastard. Could chew yer toe off. "See Mr. Rat? Acts like he owns the place."

"He does," Zam said, "in several senses."

Chucked my trainer at it. Missed.

Only when I got up did Mr. Rat scuttle off down a hole under the bog. I stuffed some pages of the *Daily Mail* in to block it off.

All the excitement wore me out.

Shut my eyes and slid downhill.

Today's outlook: overcast; rain later.

Thought 'bout Gemma, the last time Kylie brought her

to Wandsworth. She was five then. She's seven now. On the outside, time's fast and slow. Inside, it's slow. Lethally. Gem brought her new My Little Pony to Wandsworth Kylie got her for her birthday and told her was from me. Actually it was a Fake My Little Pony from a pound shop, but Gem didn't mind. She named it Blueberry Dash. She said it was basically a good pony but a bit naughty 'cause it peed in the bath.

"The things they come out with, eh?" Zam said.

Day 4. The quack said, "Mr. Wilcox, I'm Dr. Wong."

Saw Chinese eyes above his mask. My throat hurt, but it was an open goal: "I'd rather have Dr. Right."

"If I had a tenner every time I heard that, I'd be in my mansion in the Cayman Islands." He seemed all right. Took my temperature with an ear gizmo. Took my pulse. Took a swab from up my nostril. "The testing's still woefully haphazard, but I'd say you have it."

"So is it off to a clinic full of pretty nurses?"

"Half the pretty nurses are off sick, and the clinic is full. As is the overspill ward. As long as you're merely uncomfortable, you're best off roughing it out here. Believe me."

Outlook: unsettled for the rest of the day.

My hearing was weird. When Zam asked 'bout the special Covid hospital in East London, his voice sounded far-off.

"They're not admitting prisoners," Dr. Wong told me.

Pissed me off, that. "Are they afraid I'll nick my own ventilator and flog it on eBay? Or is it that us guests of Her

Majesty's hospitality don't deserve to live as much as every-one else?"

Dr. Wong shrugged. We both knew the answer. Give me six Paracetamol, six Ventolin, and a tiny bottle of codeine.

Zam said he'd make sure I followed the instructions.

"Good luck," Dr. Wong said. "I'll drop in soon."

Then me and Zam were on our own again.

Water chunders down a pipe.

Stay alert. Drink bleach.

Six fat sausages, sizzling in the pan. Tell Kylie 'bout my wacko prison nightmare. 'Bout Laverty's flat, prison, Zam, her and Gemma and Steven. God it felt so real. Kylie laughed. "Poor Lukey. . . . I don't know any Stevens." Then I'm walking Gem to school up Gilbert's End. Light greens, lush greens. Sunshine on my face. Horses running across the fringes like in *Red Dead Redemption*. Tell Gem how I went to Saint Gabriel's school, too, once upon a time. The year I stayed with my uncle Ross and aunt Dawn right here, in Black Swan Green. Mr. Pratley's still the headmaster. Ain't aged a day. He thanks me for accepting his invita-tion. I tell him how Saint Gabriel's is the only school I went to where it weren't Bully or Be Bullied. Next up, I'm in my old classroom. Here's my cousins Robbie and Em. Plus Joey Drinkwater. Sakura Yew. "It's been thirty years since the coronavirus changed our world," Mr. Pratley says, "but Luke recalls it as if it were yesterday. Isn't that right, Luke?" All eyes on me. So the virus is now a history lesson. So I'm fifty-five. Time flies on the outside. Then I see him. At the back. Arms folded. He's Him, I'm Me. No-name terms, us two. Gunshot wound in his neck's opening and closing like some underwater valve-mouth off David Attenborough. I know his face better than I know my own. Fixed. Knowing. Sad. Silent. That's the face he had bleeding out on Laverty's sofa. Half his throat was missing. It was his shooter. We was fumbling for it. Bang. Wish to fuck it hadn't happened. But if wishes was horses, beggars would ride. I wake up. Sick as a dog. Sorry as hell. Three years before the parole board even look at my paperwork. Day 5 of quarantine. Storms closing in. Thunder. Why do I have to wake up? Why? Day after day after day. Can't do this no more. Just bloody can't.

Day 6. I think. Gales. Stabs of lightning. My body's a body bag. Stuffed with pain, hot gravel, and me. Three steps to the shitter and I'm done. It hurts. Breathing hurts. Not breathing hurts. Everything bloody hurts. It's night, not day. Night 7. Night 8? Zam says I'm dehydrated. He makes me drink water. Zam must use the shitter when I'm sleeping. Tactful. Pogo Hoggins shat morning, noon, and night. Mr. Rat got to the breakfast box before me. Ate his way inside and nicked the sausage. I ain't hungry but still. Could die in here and nobody'd know till the pandemic's over. Mr. Rat would know. Mr. Rat and his hungry friends. If I died here, what'll Gem remember of me? Skinny skin-head skull in prison PJs, blubbing at her picture of Mummy, Daddy, Gemma, and Blueberry Dash. Give it a few years, even that'll fade. I'll be a name. A face on a phone that gets deleted one day. A skeleton in the cupboard. The family offender. Drugs and manslaughter. Nice. Gem's future pictures of her family'll be her, her mother, Steven, and baby brother. Not "half brother." "Brother." And yer know what?

"What?" Zam pours my codeine. "Drink."

I swallow it. "It's best for Gem she forgets me."

"How do you figure that out?"

"Who's feeding her? Clothing her? Keeping her warm in winter? Buying her her My Little Pony Magic Castle? Model Citizen Steven. Project Manager Steven. Business Studies Steven."

"Is that so, Self-Pity Studies Luke?"

"I'd belt yer one if I could lift my arm."

"Consider me belted. But doesn't Gemma get a say?"

"Next time she sees me, I'll be over thirty."

"Ancient." Zam's older. Can't tell his age.

"If, if I'm lucky, I'll be working in an Amazon slave mine. Most likely, I'll be begging outside Tesco's until I end up back here. Why'd Gemma—or any daughter—want to say, 'He's my dad'? How can I compete with Steven?"

"Don't. Concentrate on being Luke."

"Luke's an addict homeless loser sad sack."

"Luke's a lot of things. Be the best of them."

"Yer sound like an *X Factor* judge."

"Is that a good thing or bad thing?"

"It's an easy thing. Yer talk proper, Zam. Yer've got a

bank account. Education. People. Safety nets. When yer get out, yer'll have options. When I get out, I'll have my twenty-eight-quid discharge grant, and . . ." Shut my eyes. Here's Laverty's flat. Here's the bloke who'll always be dead. Dead. 'Cause of me.

"What we've done isn't who we are, Luke."

My brain's a featherweight stuck in a cage with the Hulk. He just keeps pummeling. "What are you, Zam? A fucking vicar?"

Never heard him laugh till now.

"Morning, Mr. Wilcox." Chinese eyes. A mask.

Fever's lifted. "Dr. Right."

"Caymans, here we come. Still here?"

Today's outlook: brighter patches, dry. "Ain't dead yet. Feel OK. Thanks to Nurse Zam."

"Good. Who's Sam?"

"Zam. With a zed." I point to the bunk above.

"Are we talking . . . a higher power? Or the prison governor?"

I'm baffled, he's baffled. "No. Zam. My celly."

"A cellmate? In here? During quarantine?"

"Bit late now for the shock 'n' horror, Doc. Yer met him last time. Asian bloke." I call up: "Zam! Reveal yerself."

Zam keeps shtum. Dr. Wong looks stumped. "I wouldn't have tolerated two inmates in one cell on the quarantine wing."

" 'Fraid yer bloody did tolerate it, Doc."

"I would have noticed a third person in here. There's not exactly a wealth of hiding places."

Water chunders down a toilet pipe.

I call up to Zam, "Zam, will yer just tell him?"

My cellmate doesn't reply. Asleep? A windup?

Dr. Wong looks worried. "Luke, have you had access to drugs of a more recreational nature than the ones I prescribed? I shan't tell the guards. But as your doctor, I need to know."

"This ain't funny, Zam. . . ." So I get up and stand up and find Zam's empty bed with no sheets or nothing.

SYSTEMS

BY CHARLES YU

hey need each other. Like to be around each other. Like to touch each other.

They search for things:
    Harry and meghan
    hary and megan Canada
    new year's resolutions
    new year's resolutions how long

They like being with their families. They like being with strangers. They work in small spaces. Crowd into boxes, push the air around. Sleep in boxes. Need each other. Touch each other. They move around the world. Everywhere in the world. Like us.

They search for things:
    Harry and William
    meghan and kate
    Meghan and Kate feud
    NFC playoff picture

They ask themselves:
   should I be afraid
   how afraid should I be

They ask themselves: What is coronavirus. corona virus what is it. Oscar party ideas. State of the Union. State of the Union what time. Super Bowl odds. Bean dip very spicy. Bean dip not so spicy. They ask themselves if they should be afraid but they already are.

They have patterns. Weekends. Summer plans. They have ways of doing things. They don't see how they can give those up.

They have weaknesses. They need each other. Like being around each other. They make noises. Open their mouths and push the air around and make noises at each other. Ha ha ha is a noise. Thank you is a noise. Did you see the thing about meghan and harry is a noise.

They have systems. Systems have pressure. Pressure to grow. Make more of things. More and more and more.

They go in the air boxes and in those boxes are smaller boxes and smaller boxes and many of them crawl inside a box and sit there and share the air.

Their movements seem random at first but study their movements and it becomes clear that the systems have patterns. Sunlight brings them out of their small boxes, they move together in streams. Massive streams, sometimes traveling quite far from their home boxes to hubs or centers where they collect in large boxes. Streams on the ground. They are also capable of airborne travel. They sort themselves and divide their work up. The work is to make more. More and more and more. All day long they break off in groups, then re-form new groups. Air is pushed. There is touching. In the moonlight they stream back to their boxes or to other boxes.

When it gets warmer they spend less time in boxes. When it is colder they heat up their boxes. They follow cycles of earth and moon and sun. Most of them live for many cycles.

They search for things: First date ideas. Tapas bars. Tapas downtown. Wuhan. Wuhan where. Sushi near me. How to tell if he's interested. How to tell if she's interested. Good first date how to tell. Second date ideas. Italy. Lombardy Italy. Chinese virus. Trump Chinese virus. Coronavirus versus flu. Covid not that bad.

They search for things: Why do some people say coronavirus not that bad. News sources trustworthy. Fauci. Fauci credentials. Fauci facepalm gif. Fauci handsome. Fauci married.

They divide themselves into groups. They say: Some of us are them and some of us are us. They do not always tell the truth. They spread things on their own. More and more and more.

They ask themselves:
    who invented coronavirus
    WHO invented coronavirus

They search for things: Governor. Lockdown.

They change their patterns.

They search for:
    how long is six feet

They ask themselves: Zoom what is it. How to use Zoom. School grades. Do my grades count.

They search. They look for patterns. They gather data. They look for patterns in the data and then they do something unexpected: They change their own patterns. No more streaming to large boxes. The hubs are empty. The streams are gone. The airborne migration is gone. They stay still in small boxes.

They ask themselves: Affordable Chromebooks. Does Zoom cost money. Bored kid. Activities for bored kid. Teacher thank-yous. Teacher appreciation. Green onions grow. Green onions grow how fast. Quadratic formula.

Sine cosine tangent. How to be hopeful for kids. How to seem hopeful for kids. Lockdown how much longer. What to say to kids.

Their older ones sit alone in boxes. Staring at smaller boxes. Their older ones have trouble with air.

They find patterns but some of them need to find more patterns.
   Showing results for: coronavirus
   Search instead for: coronavirus conspiracy

They ask themselves: How to cut hair. How to fix kid's haircut. Hats for kids.

The younger ones search: Interview with astronaut. Museum virtual tour. When does my school start again. Thing versus Hulk who wins. Hulk versus Thor no hammer who wins. Hulk and Thing versus Thor drunk who wins. Coronavirus real. Coronavirus kids. Mother's Day ideas. Gifts for your mom. Gifts to make for your mom no money. All the Spidermans versus Hulk who wins.

They need each other, like each other. They miss each other.

They ask themselves:
   can cats get depressed

They search for:

Food bank donation. Food bank near me.

What is a pandemic. What is furlough. How to keep kids safe. How to keep older people safe. How old is old. Am I old.

What is

How to

Is it OK

Can I

Numbers. Numbers up. Numbers growing.

How long before symptoms of coronavirus? Is there vaccine for coronavirus? How do I avoid coronavirus? How did coronavirus start? Is virus getting worse? What is mental health? How can I tell if I am depressed? What is safest takeout?

They search for:

Stop payment indicator.

what does stop payment indicator mean for unemployment

unemployment office number

when do we open up Lexington

when are we reopening Flint

when can we reopen Bowling Green

When it gets warmer they change their patterns again. They are temperature-sensitive and they spend less time in their boxes.

Many of them die. When they die, they stop pushing air. When they die they do not search for things anymore.

The weather changes and their patterns change again. Staying still in boxes for many cycles, they begin to emerge. Some of them are hungry.

Some of them are hungry. They restart the system. Slowly, the streams resume. The pressure builds. More and more and more. They make food. Some of them have too much food. Some of them share food with others. Some of them line up for food.

They search for things: cat still depressed
    are we in a bear market
    what is a bear market
    what is a payroll tax cut
    what is martial law
    how do I shelter in place
    safest cities to live
What is considered a fever. What is considered a dry cough. What is considered essential.

What is open right now. What is Marshall law. How to make hand sanitizer. How to sew a face mask. Shirt as mask. Underwear as mask. What is N95. How to break a fever. Living alone. What if I'm alone

They have subgroups. The subgroups are virtually indistinguishable. Genetically. They have invisible signals that help members of one subgroup identify fellow members. They divide themselves. They say: Some of us are us, and some of us are them.

They have weaknesses.

Some of them are aggressive. Some of them are confused. Some of them have short memories. Some of them cannot change their patterns. They have systems. Systems of air. Of information. Of ideas.

Some of them enjoy breathing as their right.

Some of them can't breathe.

Some of them send signals with incorrect information about the environment.

Misinformation spreads quickly through the population.

Misinformation can be transmitted through the mouth or eyes.

These signals confuse some of them.

Others of them study us.

They know what we are: Not quite alive. Invisible. Information.

They have invisible signals.

They talk to each other. They push air. They need each other, like each other. Miss each other. Think about each other.

They harness invisible forces. Electromagnetism. Light. They are like us. They have codes. Codes of symbolic sequences. They encode information and spread it.

They can be in small boxes and signal to each other in codes and coordinate their actions. They can be one and many and one somehow. They have particles, they have transmission, they have magical powers. They can communicate across time and space.

They have science.

They know:

Approximately 8 percent of the human genome is viral DNA.

They know we will never be apart. There are no subgroups. There is no us and them.

They search for things:

where is protest

safe to protest

how to protest

They realize:

Community is how it spreads.

Community is how it is solved.

They will keep going. Emerge from their boxes in boxes in boxes into sunlight. Cycles resuming. They will transmit messages to each other. Some of them will be confused. Some of them will share food. They will make more and more and more. Some of them will die. Some of them will be hungry. Some of them will be alone.

The systems will be the systems. But some of them may change the systems. Rebuild them. Make new patterns. They will fly again, collect again in hubs, gather by the thousands and push air at each other, ha ha ha and other noises they make to each other to signal invisible things.

Some things will not change. They will need each other. Like each other. Miss each other. They will have weaknesses. And strengths. They ask themselves: Harry and Meghan what now. Harry and Meghan what next.

THE PERFECT TRAVEL BUDDY
BY PAOLO GIORDANO

Translated by Alex Valente from the Italian

he abstinence started with Michele's arrival.

Michele is my wife's son. We haven't lived together for four years now, since he moved to Milan for college and Mavi and I moved into a smaller place, tailor-made for two.

When things started getting real bad in the north, Michele called me. I'm coming over tonight, he said.

Why?

Milan isn't safe.

But the trains must be full. And really expensive.

Trains aren't safe, either. I'm carpooling.

I objected that an infected train was still preferable to six hours in some stranger's car.

The driver has a really good rating, he said.

A couple of hours before I was supposed to pick him up, I lay down next to Mavi. I told her: I fear I've forgotten how to live with the three of us together.

I haven't, unfortunately, she replied. Can you get the lights?

But I was nervous. I couldn't let her be. We had sex, and it was over almost immediately. The air in the house had a different density. I felt a kind of pressure.

Must be the anxiety, I said on my way back from the bathroom.

Mavi seemed to have fallen asleep.

Yeah, must be the anxiety, I said again. Because of the epidemic and all.

Her hand moved gently onto my forearm. I kept it there for a while, then I got ready to leave.

I waited for Michele at the spot we'd agreed on, an empty lot outside Rome, way over the bypass. Weeds in the cracks in the asphalt and glares from people at a local bar, probably because I'd been sitting in the car for the last 30 minutes. At 3:00 a.m.

I was thinking back to other similar moments, from when Michele was 9, 10, 11. Mavi and her ex-husband always chose unhappy places like this one for their hostage exchanges. Mall parking lots, intersections. I would sit in my car pretending I wasn't there. Mavi and Michele would get in, and no one would say anything until we got home. I'd choose music carefully, not too sad but not too happy either. It never really fit.

I watched Michele take an enormous bag out of the trunk. Was he planning on staying that long? The driver stepped out, as did a young woman holding a small dog. They said their friendly goodbyes.

A couple of minutes later, now in the car, Michele was venting about her, she'd forced them to take a pointless detour around Bologna and hadn't told anyone about the dog. What if he'd been allergic?

But Michele isn't allergic to dogs. He's allergic to cats. When I took him to meet my parents he refused to step inside, insisting that the cat hair would give him an asthma attack.

After the rant he fell silent for a while. He was studying the darkness of the city outside the car window.

You don't see them outside anymore, huh? he said, eventually.

Who?

The Chinese.

When he was 9, 10, 11, Michele would refuse Ikea cutlery because, he said, they were made in China. We had never been able to remove that association between China and Ikea. We'd given up in the end; Mavi did, anyway. She'd bought him a set for his personal use, a set that said "Made in Italy."

Maybe they're not outside because it's the middle of the night, I said.

But he insisted: You have to admit I was right about them. Admit it.

I did not. I kept glancing at his hands instead, keeping track of all the parts of the car he was touching.

I ended up blurting: Have you sanitized your hands?

Of course.

Then, as if in response to my inner protest against his presence, he added: I have the highest rating on the carpooling app. As a passenger. Apparently I'm the perfect travel buddy.

A few days later, Italy was one giant red zone. No more traveling between regions, no more than 600 feet outside your own home. Everyone, no matter where they currently found themselves, had to shelter in place, including Michele. We were trapped.

As I got back from the store, I told Mavi: I could smell my breath inside the mask; it reeks a little.

She kept leafing through her magazine.

Maybe it's the lack of sunlight, I said. Not enough vitamin D, you know?

Michele walked across the kitchen shirtless. I wanted to tell him to cover up, that I didn't like him walking around like that, but it was never a good idea to talk to him just after he got up, so I didn't.

He looked heavier than me. His body seemed to take up a lot of space. Then I remembered having the same thought several years earlier, when he was a third of the size and hated me in that clear, straightforward way in which every child must hate his or her stepfather.

As soon as the bathroom door closed, I turned to Mavi: You see that? He's wearing my socks.

I gave them to him. He doesn't have any light ones.

But I care about those socks.

She looked at me oddly: You care about those socks?

I do. A little.

Don't worry, they're still washable.

Despite my efforts, I was annoyed. Because of my breath and because of my socks, though I wasn't sure which one I cared about the most. Or maybe because Mavi and I hadn't touched each other since Michele's arrival. I wasn't even sure which was the biggest factor in our drifting apart: Michele, the epidemic, or that last, disastrous attempt the evening of his arrival. At night, I'd stare at my wife's back in the dim light of the bedroom, and I'd see a ridge too high to climb.

In those moments, I'd often think back to an interview with a music star; I think I read it in *Rolling Stone* magazine, just after 9/11. The singer talked about how, confronted with the images of the towers and the smoke, he and his partner had started fucking furiously. Hours and hours on end, he said. Sex in the face of fear. An act of creation to ward off the destruction. Cosmic forces, Eros and Thanatos. That sort of stuff.

And here we were, Mavi and I. Stuck. Apart. As the world outside kept growing darker.

The socks were only the beginning. Michele's conquest would expand on multiple fronts, I knew it.

He quickly requisitioned the only Ethernet cable in the house that ensured a stable connection. For his online classes, he said. Then he took my headphones.

Earbuds are bad for him after a while, Mavi said, siding with him.

189

The only balcony in the apartment became his break room. Every day he'd line up white cigarette butts on the railing; I wouldn't refrain from counting them before throwing them in the trash. When I pointed out to him that the wind could blow them onto the downstairs balconies, he told me that was an unlikely scenario.

Finally, he asked me if he could use my home office. Before I could come up with a feasible defense, he added: It's not like you work in the evening anyway.

That was the first Friday of the lockdown. I took the time to chew my mouthful of chicken.

What do you need it for?

Houseparty.

I had no idea what he was talking about, but I said nothing. It would weaken my position.

It's quieter in your spot, Michele added.

I know. That's why it's my office.

Mavi gave me a disappointed look, so I stood up and opened the fridge, looking for nothing in particular. There was a six-pack of Tennent's Super, his supplies for the evening.

Houseparty, I mumbled.

I later turned up the volume on the TV to cover Michele's laughter and the music blaring out of his laptop's speakers. The more he enjoyed himself, the lower my mood sank.

Doesn't it make you uncomfortable to be listening in on his party? I said to Mavi.

He's letting off steam with his friends. They're all so far away, he misses them.

He could do it quietly! I almost said.

What I actually said was: It reminds me of all the nights I spent in the car waiting for him to leave a club.

Because suddenly all my years with Mavi and Michele were reduced to that: endless waiting. Waiting in front of a club, or in a parking lot; waiting in the bedroom in total silence; waiting for him to come of age so that Mavi and I could actually start living our life as a couple. Waiting to grow older so we could be young lovers. How had everything happened backward? And how had we ended up back at square one just as we thought we'd made it? I let myself wallow in that comforting wave of self-pity.

That was maybe four times, Mavi said.

I turned the volume up some more.

No, I mumbled. It was way more than four.

The following morning I carefully studied the desk's white top. The amber halos of the empty beers were still visible. I took the cleaning cloth out of the closet, making a show of it, making sure Mavi saw me.

He hasn't changed, she sighed. I'll tell him not to use your office again.

Of course not, I replied. He was only letting off steam with his friends.

Nine more Houseparty Fridays took place in my office. Nine more weeks made up of identical days and identical nights. The longest that Mavi and I hadn't had sex, without even trying. We never talked about it. If we had, we would've convinced each other that the circumstances weren't ideal. And we would've felt worse for lying.

In bed, on the 71st night, I watched her ridge-back and imagined my own *Rolling Stone* interview:

How did you react to the pandemic?

By not moving.

What's the first thing you'll do when the lockdown is lifted?

Go see an andrologist.

Every now and then I'd hear Michele's baritone laughter. He would soon be moving back to Milan for the next phase. Was the city suddenly safe? No. But as he explained, almost guiltily, he was no longer used to the three of us living together for this long. I saw the place, emptied of his presence, I saw myself lying in the same spot on the bed, and I waited for a sense of relief that never came. What I felt instead was unsettled, the feeling growing stronger by the minute.

The number of infections was falling. I'd seen the local business owners cleaning their stores, getting ready. The excitement that came with a return to life was buzzing all around me, but there I was, in my bed, hoping for an upsurge of virus infections, hoping for the lockdown to never be lifted, for the pandemic to go on forever and ever and for Michele to never go back to Milan, for him to stay up every night, having online raves at my desk. Because the alternative would be for Mavi and me to ask ourselves what happened to us, why sex was so bad the last time and non-existent since. Why we hadn't had sex in the face of fear.

The window was open, but I suddenly found myself gasping for air. I pulled off the sheet and sat up.

Can't sleep? Mavi asked me from her remote corner of the bed.

I'm thirsty.

I headed to the kitchen. Michele was there. Eating ice cream out of the tub. I took out a glass, filled it with water, and sat down in front of him.

No Houseparty? I asked.

I didn't feel like it.

As always, he hadn't waited for the ice cream to thaw, so he was stabbing the spoon forcefully into the tub. I was about to tell him that he'd bend the metal that way. And that he was using an Ikea spoon without any complaints, but I chose to remain silent.

I met a girl, he said. We went to a private room. She wanted to . . . yeah. But I didn't feel like it.

He didn't look at me. If he had, he would have seen my confusion, not at the conversation itself, but at having never thought of the possibility until that very moment of meeting someone in these circumstances, during a lockdown, on Houseparty, and even having sex with them. And yet, as he said it, with the naive brightness of his 22 years, it felt perfectly natural.

I liked her, but I'm a little more complicated, he continued. Screens make me anxious for this sort of thing. To each their own, you know?

Without waiting for a reply, he nudged the ice cream in my direction.

You can finish it, he said. It's salted caramel, the best flavor if you ask me.

I stared at the spoon streaked with cream and saliva. Extremely high risk of contagion. I wanted to stand up and grab a clean one, but Michele was looking at me, innocently. So I took the spoon, brought it to my lips. Once, then again.

You always clean the sides, huh? he pointed out. I never care. I just go for the middle.

He left. I finished the ice cream; not that there was that much left. Then I headed back to bed.

What took you so long? Mavi asked.

Nothing. Just had some ice cream.

I raised my hand to her ridge-back. I grazed the middle, just beneath the soft creases of her top.

That's ticklish, she said.

Want me to stop?

No.

AN OBLIGING ROBBER BY MIA ❋ COUTO

Translated by David Brookshaw from the Portuguese

here's a knock on the door. Well, "knock" is one way of describing it. I live far away from anyone; war and famine are my only visitors. And now, in the eternity of yet another afternoon, someone bombards the door with his feet. I run over. Well, "run" is one way of putting it. I drag my feet, my slippers creaking over the wooden floor. At my age, that's all I can do. Folks start to age when they look at the ground and see an abyss.

I open the door. It's a masked man. On noting my presence, he shouts:

"Six feet, keep six feet away!"

If he's a robber, he's frightened. His fear unnerves me. Frightened robbers are the most dangerous ones. He takes a pistol from his pocket. He points it at me. But it's a funny-looking weapon: It's made of white plastic and emits a green light. He points the pistol at my face, and I close my eyes, obedient. That light on my face is almost a caress. To die like this is a sign that God has answered my prayers.

The masked man is soft-spoken and has an affable look. But I'm not letting myself be fooled: The cruelest of soldiers always approached me with an angel's demeanor. But it has been so long since I had any company at all that I end up playing his game.

I ask the visitor to lower his pistol and take a seat in the only chair I have left. It's only then that I notice his shoes are wrapped in some sort of plastic bags. His intentions are clear: He doesn't want to leave any footprints. I ask him to take his mask off and assure him that he can trust me. The man smiles sadly and mumbles: These days one can't trust anyone, people don't know what they're carrying inside them. I understand his enigmatic message; the man thinks that underneath my wretched appearance, there lies hidden a priceless treasure.

He looks around, and as he can't find anything to steal, he eventually explains himself. He says he's from the health services. And I smile. He's a young robber; he doesn't know how to lie. He tells me his bosses are worried because of a serious illness that's spreading like wildfire. I pretend to believe him. I almost died of smallpox. Did anyone visit me? My wife died of tuberculosis, did anyone come and see us? Malaria took my only son, and I was the one who buried him. My neighbors died of AIDS, and no one wanted to know about it. My late wife used to say it was our fault because we chose to live far from where there were any hospitals. She, poor soul, didn't know that it was the other way around. It is hospitals that are built far from the poor.

It's just the way hospitals are. I don't blame them. I'm like them, hospitals I mean; I'm the one who harbors and tends to my own illnesses.

The lying robber doesn't give up. He refines his methods, though still in a clumsy way. He tries to justify himself: The pistol he pointed at me was to measure my fever. He says I'm well, announcing this with an idiotic smile. And I pretend to breathe a sigh of relief. He wants to know whether I have a cough. I smile disdainfully. A cough is something that almost sent me to my grave, after I came back from the mines 20 years ago. Ever since then, my ribs have hardly moved, and nowadays my chest just consists of dust and rock. The day I cough again, it will be to attract St. Peter's attention at heaven's gate.

"You don't seem ill to me," the impostor declares. "But you may be an asymptomatic carrier."

"A carrier?" I ask. "A carrier of what? For the love of God, you can search my house, I'm an honorable man, I hardly ever leave home."

The visitor smiles and asks if I can read. I shrug. Then he places a document on the table with instructions on how to maintain hygiene, along with a box containing cakes of soap, and a small bottle of what he calls "an alcohol-based solution." Poor fellow, he must imagine I'm partial to liquor, like all lonely old men. As the intruder takes his leave, he says:

"In a week's time, I'll come by and see you."

At this point, the name of this illness the visitor is talking about dawns on me. I know the illness well. It's called indifference. They would need a hospital the size of the whole world to treat this epidemic.

Disobeying his instructions, I advance toward him and give him a hug. The man resists me vigorously and wriggles out of my arms. Back in his car, he hurriedly strips off. He frees himself from his clothes as if he were stripping himself of the plague's own attire. That plague called poverty.

I wave goodbye and smile. After years of torment, I am reconciled with humanity: Such a bumbling robber can only be a good man. When he comes back next week, I'll let him steal that old television I've got in my bedroom.

SLEEP * BY UZODINMA IWEALA

he day I awake? Tomorrow, yes—Wednesday—and feel nothing beside me, then fleeting feelings of betrayal, then indignation—obviously righteous. Tomorrow will make today yesterday, just another day, not that day to be remembered forever, not that special day marked always on my finger. Maybe as big, bright and shining, maybe subtle and elegant, maybe not on my finger at all. Maybe just a thought—security. Just a thought—happiness. Just a thought—love. Just a thought—forever—that will be remembered before all those moments, those past moments, those precious moments we've shared. Those smiles, hugs, kisses, couplings—so many couplings.

Tomorrow in the soft summer sunlight I will stir, feel warmth on my face, feel warmth on my body, feel the cool dry air that the air-conditioning brings. Light, bright and clear, cast on your empty pillow will show your hair growing out from the slip like little black curly sprouts. You will be going bald early. It's the stress, and so you know, I'll still love you when it's all gone. When I am all gone. I will smile—no, laugh—and spread my body over your still-warm indentation to see if by being where you were

203

I can be you. No such luck. Tough luck. I never liked our sheets—your sheets—because of how they grow so cold so quick when you are gone.

I will be alone again, with only my thoughts, with only my longing, with only my insecurities and a whole host of melancholy things. And I will think, So this is the depth of reconciliation. Return to the status quo? You off to work before the dawn, leaving only a trace of your presence—the waning heat in the bed beside me, and me again alone wondering if life could be better, if life will be better perhaps officially coupled and recognized by the state, by God or by gods. Yes, you and me joined. Yes, me somehow officially complete. But tomorrow, I fear, like today, like yesterday, will bring no such luck, and I will think I never liked our sheets—your sheets—because they are the green of your hospital scrubs and remind me that for you to work is to live, to live is to suffer and a whole host of melancholy things.

I will get up and feel sunlight on my breasts, feel sunlight on my stomach, feel sunlight on the neatly shaved triangle between my legs. And with this light will come thoughts of missed opportunity the previous night, fleeting feelings of lust, then longing—your flesh my flesh, you and me joined, yes me, for a moment, somehow officially complete. But that will all be yesterday, tomorrow will be today, and I will walk from bed to bathroom thinking I live in spurts—perhaps that's why you can't marry me. Perhaps we are too incompatible.

The whole room is my spurts—the paintings on your walls, modern prints of ancient art, originals from artist friends and my clothes tossed over various pieces of furniture, a shirt on the old brown leather easy chair, jeans by the foot of the bed, panties by the wastebasket. All these spurts right to the bathroom and its tarnished, brass-rimmed mirror that I found, that you hated, that I loved, the one that makes you feel as if it is 70 years before present and you are a scratched-up picture of a Negro steward in your own home. No such luck. Wonderful luck. You never liked our history—my history—because of how it makes kings into servants and madmen into kings.

I will look at the mirror, and I will think I am tired of hearing you say you want to change it. And I will look in the mirror, at myself, at the fine wrinkles on my eyelids, at the light crow's feet near the corners of my eyes, and I will look down past the dimple of my belly button to the space free of hair and so sensitive it turns red where fingers have touched just above the triangle between my legs, and I will place my palm on this spot, imagine a kick, and think, Toby—I'm not getting any younger. I will mumble, There is no forever here.

I will look at the mirror and I will think soon you will be able to change it. And I will look in the mirror, at my white face, now red, tear-streaked, and horrible, look at the blood vessels broken beneath the surface, and think— I have color at least. And then I will look at my white face, now red, tear-streaked, and horrible, look at the blood vessels broken beneath the surface and think, Toby, am I only white to you?

On bad days—always. On good days—sometimes. Then there are spectacular moments.

I will say to myself, Poor thing, you, and stand there fully naked, arms crossed over my breasts, holding myself, watching me watch me wonder, Toby, am I only white to you? I will say, Ashley, come on. Get dressed. You can't carry on like this. Like what, I will ask. Like this, I will say, paralyzing yourself, dramatizing your life. If you love him, don't leave him, and if you leave him this time, leave him alone. There are other relationships. I will sit down on the bed where you lay and I will think there will never be another you. I will say, But I'm scared, in a voice an octave away from being unheard.

I will shower, drip water from my hair onto the floor, onto the bed, across the carpets, to the dresser—the mahogany one that your father's mother gave your mother that I hoped your mother would one day give to me. No such luck. Tough luck. I will lay my body on your still-warm indentation to see if by being where you were I will somehow realize that I should be with you. No such luck. Tough luck. I will mumble, I never liked our sheets—your sheets. I will mumble, Break the cycle. There is too much history here.

That will be tomorrow, but this night, above the sirens, and the helicopters, and the heated chants, for a time you breathe rhythmically and I breathe in spurts. You on top of me. Your body next to me. Sweat smell, sex smell, and all the feelings—your skin beneath my nails, your hand around my throat. Toby. Stop, I tell you, stop. Why? you ask me, why?

Because now there is something hard between us.

Toby, answer me truthfully, I say. Toby, do you ever think of marrying me? Silence from you. From you no noise. Just your hot breath and that hardness between us. Toby, I say. I ask Toby, Am I only white to you? Silence. Shifting. You tucked between your legs.

I think bad days. I think good days. I think there are spectacular moments. I think tears. I think smiles. I think love and the life it should bring. But that is all future. In the past it was all different—I think.

Then, I said, As you wish. Let us sleep. You hung up and I hung up and I found myself alone again. I put my palms behind my head and reclined into these sheets once warmed by your body and wrinkled, once tangled because of you and aggravatingly positioned in all the wrong places— a knot under my chin, a bunch between my legs—now flat, uninspired and uninspiring. I put a pillow in your place and wrapped the sheets around it, thinking, At least if it lay where you were, then I would dream it was you. I did not and when the sunlight warmed my eyelids into a brilliant orange, I woke and thought, Oh, shit, I'm late. I'm screwed.

I swung my feet over the edge of the bed onto the floor, not onto books, or shoes, or underwear, or shirts or pens, and I was again relieved that I had damaged nothing, scattered nothing, that my phone would display no messages about my maltreatment of your existence. I should have been happy, but in this space, the absence of your things made me think of standing above you while you slept, as your light, quick breaths troubled your lips. You, the mystical, the magical, my love, my life. How I would think—Are you really my love my life? And then, There are no easy answers here.

I brushed my teeth quickly, but when I spat out, the white foam around the drain refused to drain. I turned on the water, and there were still white bubbles. I pulled the drain plug and hanging on its ends were strands of your hair, wet and twisted together, slowing the progress of my day. I shivered and flung the whole thing into the wastebasket. Then I washed my face, examined my imperfections in your mirror, and rushed out the front door.

Imagine my surprise when I found you sitting in the hallway. I didn't want to wake you, you said. I looked at you again, turned to the door and back to you there, your arms on your knees and a silent please that stretched wide your eyes, nostrils, and lips. Your horrid half smile.

You reached out to me and I reached out to you across the divide of the hallway, through the sunlit dust particles that danced in slow currents from the central air. Your white hands, my Black hands, then clasped hands and then a hug. I felt you breathe against me, and I wondered— affection, comfort, desire, or all of these things—as your stomach touched mine and as we kissed and you tasted of the day before. I didn't care, couldn't care, and you pushed me back into the apartment. You brought your hands to my face and held my cheeks. You said, I want you, Toby. I felt your hands on my chest, on my stomach, then lower still, coaxing, caressing, and I thought you naked here on the floor, me naked here on the floor, us naked together. I was overwhelmed by the onslaught, confused. I said to you, Stop, Ashley, stop. Why, you asked me, why?

Because you always disappear when there is something hard between us.

Because I'm already late for work, I said.

Right, you said. Toby. It's me. Ashley—your once and future girlfriend, the mystical, the magical, your love your life, the one you begged to come back last night. Aren't you happy to see me?

Happy to see you? At the moment, I said yes, and I believed myself. Happy to see you—of course yes. No more returning to this home empty of you and yet filled with your presence—your hairs on the pillow beside mine, in my hair and hairbrush, around the sink your deodorant, lotions, perfumes, and a whole host of lavender-scented things. Happy to see you? Yes of course because it was too much to have you here and not have you. Too perfect— at some points exactly what I had wished for—too absurd.

I'm just surprised. I didn't think you would come, I said. But I came, you said. You pressed up against me so that we rattled the coat-closet door. You slid your fingers down my chest and whispered, I'll be waiting for you when you get home. I love you.

I said, I love you, too, Ashley.

I couldn't concentrate at the hospital, but everyone considered my confusion a result of the overwhelming responsibility and complexity of the times. The attending, with his curly brown hair and its white wisps falling down over his glasses, put a palm on my shoulder and in a quiet moment said, This is not forever. This, too, shall pass. He said, Where there are humans, there is hope. I wanted to believe him, but I was distracted by my thoughts of you.

I came home to you sitting in the darkness on the edge of the bed staring out the open window. I need to shower, I said. You said nothing. When I emerged, towel around my waist, water streaked down the hard-to-reach regions of my spine, you asked, Can you hear them shouting? I pulled you up from the bed and kissed you. I swept my hands up your long white legs, skin so pale as to show the blue veins branched like lightning beneath. I shivered—from excitement, from disgust? I lifted your tank top to reveal the dimple in your navel, to reveal your bra's red imprints just beneath your breasts and the freckles around your nipples. You kicked your panties toward the wastebasket and pulled me to you. And now, I breathe rhythmically and you breathe in spurts until you tell me, Stop. You say, Stop.

Why, I ask you, why?

Silence from you, from you no noise, and I think, Because now there is something hard between us. And now that we lie like this—facing each other, you aware of my excitement, me aware of my excitement, you unwilling to make love, me unwilling to resist the urge—both staring into the darkness while the world burns, I think forget love, forget passion, forget sexual reconciliation and all the intimate things. I think, then, As you wish, let us sleep.

Toby, answer me truthfully, you say. Toby, do you ever think of marrying me? And then you whisper, Am I only white to you?

You always ask questions like this because you think the answers are simple, that I can first say yes and then say no, that I will learn to let love conquer the thousand-year hate and other hard things between us.

Once, you could go to jail and I could go to jail for what we are doing now. Once, they would have strung me from a tree, slit my scrotum, and let gravity unravel my testicles.

But that is all past—I think. In the future, it will all be different—I think.

THE ✹ CELLAR
BY DINA NAYERI

his is nothing," Kamran said on the night before Paris was to retreat indoors.

Sheila looked up from their walking forms. "I refuse to show papers to police." Glancing at Nushin, she whispered, "They're always young . . . just boys with guns they can hardly lift."

History, Kamran reminded them, had trained them for lockdowns and famines and power-drunk police. Pandemic or not, they were still on sabbatical. They'd enjoy their new city, minus a few restaurant meals. They'd revive the window geraniums, air out the landlord's musty linens. "And look at that sky, like a ripe grapefruit. Nothing can ruin a sky like that."

"What's next . . . dress codes? Mullahs? Woman-check?" Sheila muttered, remembering bygone humiliations as she wrote false birthdays and dropped a digit from their door number.

"Daddy," Nushin said, freshly vigilant at four. "If we don't go out, we'll get peeled!"

The daily death tolls reminded Kamran and Sheila of wartime Tehran, in the '80s, when they were barely out of

215

childhood, pockets still sticky from tamarind, though they made a somber show of checking the BBC each night for casualty numbers, like adults. The Islamic Republic news lied so consistently that Kamran and Sheila no longer blamed or counted on it. They simply waited for their fathers to tune the radio to the BBC, and struggled not to glance sidelong at each other.

Privately, each suspected the coronavirus numbers too, indulging in brief spells of imagination for which they blamed the revolution and a childhood at war. Kamran joked that modern Iranians were lucky, because once again, they had fake death tolls to keep them happy. And yet, each night they dutifully reminded each other that the BBC knows.

They made fun of friends panicking over pasta and bread. "Amateurs," Kamran said. "Rationing would give them a collective aneurysm." Once, at the start of the war, Kamran remembered, his father went out for milk and came home with three flyswatters, a can of mosquito spray, a shovel, and fishhooks. The shop owner was bundling.

"I miss those days," Sheila sighed, then caught herself. "I mean, not . . ."

"Me, too," Kamran said. Then he paused. "There's a finished basement," he said, "and a cellar." He smiled, bawdy and insinuating, a Kamran from another life. The suggestion drummed at her heart, quickening everything.

For days, they stumbled into warrens of memory as they postured better responses for Nushin. They built blanket forts, clapped for tired workers, shed tears for their ravaged country. It tore at Sheila to imagine those sinister fanged globules skewering her mother's cells. Stuck in a Tehran apartment, dependent on neighbors, this might be the way she'd lose her maman.

They browsed the shelves for distraction. The apartment creaked under a mountain of worn but respectable books in Polish and French, Miłosz's and Szymborska's poems, Bruno Schulz, Simone Weil, a surprising assortment on military strategy, Chinese medicine, and the history of maps. They squandered the hours, succumbing to the truth that, after years of academic frenzy in New York, they had wanted this. The new tension troubled and thrilled them, as it did decades ago. They carried it with them, fragile and alive like a caught fish, through the day's newfound tediums.

One morning Sheila was running her fingers across a shiny black picture book, trying to read the gold looping letters above a fairy-tale scene, when the egg timer rang. Taking it for a volume of children's stories, she carried it to the table. Nushin was well into Chapter 1 when Kamran wandered in. "So, she's too young for *Mulan*, but ancient French porn is OK?"

Sheila grabbed the book from her daughter. *The Five Senses of Eros*. Below the title, a girl with a Snow White face and whimsical curls lay on the grass, petticoats pulled back as she was meticulously tended with an ornate feather by some kind of jaunty Pan creature. Sheila stared, flushed, egg yolk oozing onto her hand, for a long time.

"Does the princess have a tummy ache?" Nushin said, craning for a better view.

Kamran turned to the inside cover. "Nineteen eighty-eight. The French were publishing this while mullahs were telling us it's halal to fall on top of your aunt during an earthquake." After the revolution, clerics appeared on television to offer practical applications of Islam. It was weirdly (almost lovingly) thorough. Stepping into a squat toilet, they advised, go left foot first so, in case of a heart attack, you won't fall into the hole. "We barely knew our own equipment, remember?"

In the afternoon, they stumbled into each other in the hallway. Still embarrassed, Sheila looked away, but he pulled her close, his warm cheek against hers. "You haven't been outside in ten days," he whispered into her hair. "You'll get peeled." She hardly registered this forgotten intimacy when they were flogged by a furious, "No!" Nushin stood huffing and glaring in the bathroom doorway, underpants around her ankles, clutching her skirt.

"You can't kiss her!" she said, lips trembling, tears welling. "She's not the princess." Her small chest heaved, as if in shock. Twice she whispered, "Say sorry to me."

Thinking of her budding dignity, Sheila rushed to pull up her daughter's pants. "Less than two weeks indoors," she whispered, "and we've permanently fucked with her sexual wiring."

"Our parents fucked with ours," Kamran said as he picked up their daughter.

Had Nushin ever seen them in love? Sheila was too ashamed to ask. They had toiled side by side for years, each with careers, postdocs, friends. After marriage, then after Nushin, sex fell away so quietly. Without oppressors or a tangible struggle, it lost its revolutionary heat.

That night, after Nushin was tucked in bed, Kamran turned to Sheila and said, "Want to tell stories from last time?" And she said, "I think my stories are wrong for now." All day she had craved to sit alone for a while and think about being 15 in a bomb shelter.

Instead Kamran recalled the day, at 13, they went walking in the streets of Tehran. A teenage pasdar berated them for an hour before Kamran convinced him they were cousins. They walked home near tears, unable to comfort each other, Kamran a few steps ahead as Sheila fumed about the upturned world, her mandatory hijab, the mere boy chastising her as if he were her father. Then they stood in the lobby, staring at their scuffed shoes, until bomb sirens blared and neighbors streamed to the basement, lifting them in a tide of parents, honorary aunts and uncles, and a lame grandmother grasping her chador as she was carried down in her son's arms.

Sheila breathed out. "Then we found the cellar." And, with it, kinship over their faulty responses, the body's terrible choice to succumb to shelter, to come alive in times of death and mourning. He kissed her palms. "Stay in. Tomorrow I'll buy you vitamin D."

• • •

"Do you remember how the old women furnished the bomb shelters?" she asked, imagining the basement under her feet—did French cellars smell like sugar and fire-warmed earth, like the ones back home, or were they full of cobwebs and caked boot prints? "Do you remember the stairs?" A jar of torshi on every step. Fat and thin canning jars, with fabric tops screwed under lids, lined up like Arab princes awaiting their turn.

"I miss the grandmas. Heaven forbid, in the middle of a war, we run out of pickle."

"I'm going to grow out my eyebrows during lockdown," Sheila said.

"You have beautiful eyebrows," Kamran said. He held her cheeks in his palms and ran his thumbs over them, as if he were applying sunscreen.

"Remember how I had to take it off three hairs at a time to fool Baba?" Nice girls didn't remove a single hair from their bodies until their wedding. So, Sheila had conspired with her mother to hide her thinning eyebrows from the building's many vigilant fathers and brothers. If a huge black swath disappears from your head, even the dumbest man knows. But if the hairs fall out one by one, we can say anything we want. We'll start a rumor: Poor girl has a hypothyroid.

Oh, Maman, please hold out . . . believe the numbers . . . stay inside.

"The last time, after the cellar," Sheila said, "my parents screamed at me for three hours."

"Mine kept fretting I'd be sent to war," Kamran said.

How had they lost track of each other for so long? "Life without war," Kamran said.

"That's awful," she said. "That's not us."

"I think maybe it is. We're hardwired for disaster."

Their two buildings were connected by an enormous basement shelter, two sets of stairs joining down in a damp cavern. Circling the room, bicycles were wedged among a dozen fridges and freezers, all stocked with cooked meals and ingredients. Shelves sagged under cans, rice, flour, sugar. Huge pots of torshi with family labels were crammed atop each fridge.

At the start of the war, the grandmothers hauled down chairs, pillows, bright floor cloths, soft quilts, and fuzzy blankets. They brought samovars, plates, cups, outfitting the shelter for meals or tea, backgammon or a smoke, so that every siren could be the start of an occasion. Among the residents lived five teenagers, including Sheila and Kamran, the two youngest and most studious, and therefore the least watched. During that first red siren, as the families fretted over pipes and samovars, arranging pillows and opining on space heaters, the two found a tunnel leading to a small cellar. Inside its rocky walls were shelves of cheeses and dry goods, packets of chopped herbs, a door that closed and enough space for two twiggy fugitives.

After that, every red siren brought them back to the cellar, in snatches of time between their fathers' rounds of chess, their grandmothers' bawdy jokes, and a thousand cups of chai.

"Do you remember the thing that saved us?" Kamran asked.

"Philadelphia." American cream cheese was rare. Even with ration coupons, people were always fighting over it, running to black markets for it. Most evenings, brave parents questing for the special cheese returned with heads hung and a packet of Laughing Cow, or worse, ordinary Iranian feta. When Kamran and Sheila heard the clip-clopping of mothers' heels, they hardly had time to throw Sheila's dress back on, tucking her bra (a self-delusional thing made entirely of cotton, no cups or wire) in Kamran's pocket. They smoothed their hair and stood far apart, but they'd still be caught together, alone in the room. They needed to offer themselves in a crime, a bad one, though not as bad as the one they'd committed. So, Kamran grabbed a packet of precious Philadelphia from a neighbor's shelf, tore past cardboard and foil and bit into a block of smooth milky white, and tossed it to Sheila. "God, this is good," she muttered, just as the mothers walked in and started screaming about stolen cheese.

"These children! *Ei vai*! They're animals," the mothers said.

All evening there were apologies. The owners of the cheese were gracious. Please. They're just children. Kamran's father offered thrice the value in coupons and cash, and they shared out the uneaten portion on crackers. Wild children. No one thought what else they might be doing there, and so they did it again and again, until they were 14, then 15, and Sheila's black eyebrows thinned and her lips filled out, Kamran's legs grew long and the mothers began envying such a son. In those years, no one told them about sex. The media tried to turn the boys' urges toward war, and to snuff out the girls' under cloth. But the young smuggled magazines, photos, an education, and cellars and larders and butteries across the city rustled and clanged with the efforts of self-taught teenagers.

Every time the siren screamed a red alert, and the din of families darting to basements filled the streets, Sheila and Kamran ran into the cellar together. Every time the alert was downgraded by a shade or two, when the neighbors sighed in relief, they pounded their pillows, beseeching that bastard Saddam to have a heart and threaten a missile just one more time. They waited for that red alert until fear and desire merged into a single strange and unthinkable brew, until bras became wiry and no longer fit into pockets, and stolen cheese became stolen cigarettes, then a taste of Grandma's moonshine or opium tea, then stopped working as an excuse, because the pair were too beautiful and cunning, and they looked at each other as if their young teeth, still milky and serrated like a bread knife, might soon sink into a leg of lamb.

In late April, Kamran found his old Kiarostami DVDs, and they watched *Taste of Cherry*. He asked why she hated remembering, even though she, too, was obviously traveling back there.

So, she told him. That her mother had checked every hair on Sheila's body for months. That she regretted conspiring together. That her parents dragged her to a specialist to sew her back up, relenting only after the specialist advised them to wait until just before marriage, to avoid having to do it twice. "It was a humiliating year. Then we left for university."

"I'm sorry," he said. He held her fingers. "It wasn't fair. All their shit rolled onto you."

In the morning Kamran took Nushin for groceries. "I'm touching zero surfaces, Daddy."

Sheila listened to the BBC. French borders had closed. This was home for now. Lockdowns across Europe would last through April, even May. They'd watch many more grapefruit sunsets from their pretty windows, no tape obstructing their view. Soon spring leaves would appear on the trees beyond the glass. But Sheila wouldn't go outside again, not for a long time. Not while French pasdars, boys still, roamed with guns, barking for papers.

She sat on the carpet for a long time, thinking of the grandmothers who made parties out of missile strikes, altering the children's memories. Maybe they meant to prepare them for hardship and war, to mangle their instincts and fuse every sensation with its opposite. Her girlish eyebrows were growing back. She craved the taste of cherry, songs from childhood, a hearty meal stolen from the chaos. Sheila pulled herself off the floor and opened the closet where she had stuffed the landlord's musty blankets. Their stench, the indignities of another era, tainted the air. She texted Kamran, took a stack of pillows, half a bottle of red, crackers, and a book, and ran to the basement to wait out the daylight.

THAT TIME AT MY BROTHER'S WEDDING
BY LAILA LALAMI

ou seem lost, Miss. Are you looking for the American consulate station? I could tell, you see, by your hat and backpack and the documents you hold tight to your chest. It's true that petty theft can be a risk in Casablanca, but I assure you the airport is a secure building. No one will take your papers away. Sit, sit. At a distance, of course, we both know the rules. Make yourself comfortable. It will be a few hours before the consular officers arrive, and, even then, it will take them a while to set up their table and start clearing passengers for departure.

How long have I been waiting? A long time, I'm sorry to say. These repatriation flights are for citizens only and—if space allows—residents. But apparently space has not allowed, at least not for the last two weeks. Every time I've put in a request, I've gotten the same answer: "Sorry, Ms. Bensaïd, the flight is full." I thought of trying the airport in Tangier, but train service is closed, and in any case there are probably more people waiting there than here. The consular officers keep telling me I should be patient, I will have better luck next time.

The thing is, it was luck that brought me here in March.

Ordinarily, I visit my family in the summer, when I am off from teaching, but early this year my brother announced that he was getting married. His fourth time, can you imagine? He scheduled the ceremony smack dab in the middle of my spring break, just to counter what he knew would be my immediate objection. Even so, I told him I couldn't attend because I had plans to go to Texas with my bird-watching group. But he's always had a knack for making me feel guilty. He brought up how thrilled our mother would be to see me, how she's getting on in years, how I should take every chance I get to spend some time with her. I couldn't say no to that.

Still, I was disappointed that my plans had been disrupted, so I scheduled a short trip to Merja Zerga, 140 miles north from here. Have you been? Oh, you'll have to visit someday. It's a tidal lagoon, a Ramsar-designated site in fact, home to an impressive variety of bird species. I wanted to see waders and marsh owls and, with any luck, flamingoes and marbled teals, which migrate through the area this time of year.

Before that, of course, I had to suffer through the wedding. It's not that I don't want to see my brother happy, you understand, it's just that he has terrible taste in women. All of them young, naive, and in awe of him. At the ceremony—invariably a lavish celebration that saddled his in-laws with debt—he would stand beside his new wife as if he were posing for a fashion magazine. My role was to be the dowdy older sister, completing the family tableau by standing in the background, slightly out of focus.

I had played the part often enough that I arrived at the

ceremony ready to take my cues. There were a hundred guests this time, a modest number by my brother's standards, but still enough that it took a long time to make the rounds, being introduced to people and exchanging congratulations and well wishes. The bride's parents were full of questions. "You live in California?" the father asked me.

"Yes," I said. "In Berkeley."

"And what do you teach?"

"Computer science," my mother replied for me. It's a point of pride for her, I think, because initially I said I wanted to be a painter, which she found impractical.

The father's eyes widened, and there was a murmur as the news traveled to the aunts and uncles and cousins who stood nearby. California, someone whispered. Berkeley. But the bride was unimpressed; she peered at me with unbounded pity. "How hard it must be for you," she said. Her voice was a squawk. Standing beside her, my brother nodded in agreement.

"What do you mean?" I asked.

"Living so far away."

"Living anywhere can be hard." Wait till you've lived with my dear brother, I thought, and then we'll see who finds life so difficult.

But her attention was already drawn elsewhere. "The photographers are here," she said.

We posed for pictures—the bride and the groom and their families and friends, in different permutations. I started to feel hot flashes coming on, even though I was in a sleeveless gown instead of a heavy caftan. I was rummaging through my purse for my hormone pills when the bride motioned for me to step out of the frame. "Now, let's do one with Moroccans only."

Can you believe it? I was about to say something sharp when my brother intervened. His new wife didn't mean anything bad, he said, it was only that the color of my dress clashed with her caftan. He pulled me back into the frame, beaming his bleach-white smile for the photographers. But I don't think he minded it all that much. Deep down he resents me because I left home at 18, while he lives in the house we grew up in, taking care of our mother. Maybe things between us would be different if he'd stayed single like me, instead of flitting from wife to wife every few years.

With all the commotion, I forgot to take my pills. After a few more minutes under the photographers' lights, I got dizzy and tumbled down, catching the bride's train to steady myself. The last thing I heard before I passed out was the flutter of the fabric as it fell to the floor.

The next day, I was preparing for my trip to Merja Zerga, feeling profound thrill at the thought of being on a boat in the lagoon, when I received word that Morocco was closing its borders. I rushed here to try to find a seat on an outbound flight, but no luck so far. Speaking of which, here come the consular officers. I recognize the young man in the blue shirt. He was here two days ago. He's already walking in this direction; he must have noticed the blue passport in your hand. Go on. Perhaps I'll see you on the other side.

THE TIME OF DEATH, THE DEATH OF TIME
BY JULIÁN FUKS

nd then, at some indefinable moment between the first rays of dawn and the dazzling light of midday, time stopped making sense. There was no fanfare, there was no noise, no din to announce something so atypical. You might have imagined clocks paralyzed, calendars muddled up, days and nights melding into one another and tingeing the sky gray, but there was none of that. Time stripped of meaning was a collective happening, and yet a strictly intimate one. It prompted nothing more than torpor, indifference, a peculiar and profound kind of despondency.

It is hard to conceive of the variety of ways the non-existence of time affected each home, each individual detained in an infinite hour. Some increased the pace of their trivial tasks, covering up the silence with automated actions, washing their hands incessantly, obsessively cleaning living rooms, kitchens, bathrooms. Others couldn't stop the torpor from taking hold of their bodies, and remained sprawled on their sofas, inert and impotent—following with vague attention the news that is always the same, the whole mathematics of tragedy. It was still possible that some relic of time might yet allow itself to be measured, not in minutes, hours, days, but in the accumulation of deaths on the television graphics.

I watched everything from the window, letting my gaze wander among the neighboring apartments, distracting myself with that life in the gaps that the landscape offered me. At the exact moment of the death of time, if I remember correctly, I was lying in the hammock staring out over nothing but empty streets. I felt that moment straying from the previous one and the next, becoming eternalized in its insignificance, gaining weight. The present swelled, as if its bulky figure became so fat that it obscured the past and blocked out the view of the whole future. Even very recent days, sunny days of liberty and innocence, now seemed to exist only as distant memories, laden with nostalgia, on the edge of forgetting. As for the future, it was so uncertain that it canceled itself completely, rendering foolish any plan I might hatch, any love I might covet, any book I might long to write. The paralysis of time, I understood, overtook houses and bodies at once, condemning to immobility legs, and arms, and hands, and existence.

On that day, or on some other, Brazil tallied 1,001 deaths. I suppose the symbolism of the number contributed to the failure of time, stealing even the fatal hands of its clocks, exhausting the final unit of measurement. The 1,001 deaths were like the 1,001 nights; they were 1,000 deaths and a death; they were infinite deaths plus one; they were infinite deaths. A whole population was discovering, in one interminable moment, that it was possible to experience in life the extemporaneous nature of death. That it was not necessary to experience pain and unhappiness to find oneself outside of time, that the imminence of pain and of happiness was enough—it was enough that this imminence become broad and impersonal for the whole temporal order to collapse.

And then, when no further measuring was possible, when everything was bewilderment and fear and boredom, I noted that it didn't take long for the opportunists to show up, those who wanted to make an old time out of the absence of time. Bit by bit, even though everything was assimilated into a single moment, the faces most commonly seen in the newspapers began to take on sinister features, their voices turning darker, their expressions coming to resemble, more and more, those from other decades. Anyone who looked closely could see in the country's highest authorities the almost grotesque image of figures from another time— under their suits, the outline of uniforms; in the shadow of their shoes, the shape of jackboots; in their hands, pens as long as nightsticks.

Hearing them could cause more desperation than examining their gestures and clothes. Their statements were the echo of other statements, ever outlandish and violent. They started off by scorning deaths and preventive measures, and contradicting scientific research, and preaching the use of an elixir capable of eliminating the pandemic. They proceeded to the need to resume work whatever the consequences, the desire to be productive and to cut wages and to pull down the forest and thereby open up land for growing. They culminated, always, in the persecution of any voice that rose up against them, in the direct assault on critics and dissidents, in the urge to subjugate their political enemies, all of them communists, terrorists, subversives.

When they fell quiet, there was something that was more than silence. On that day, or on some other, there were in me the beginnings of claustrophobia and the irrepressible need to get away, abruptly. Leave behind the apartment in which I had shut myself up, leave behind that collective inertia into which I had passively and unwittingly subsumed myself. I remember walking quickly along the streets, and how my steps seemed to be producing seconds, restoring the pulse of time to existence. I remember feeling some hostility in the empty streets, in the shadows lengthening ominously, as if something dark and ancient might attack me on any corner. Still, I longed to see somebody's face, the face of somebody who was not me, of whomever, somebody unknown, a stranger—any human face stripped of its mask or its window would be enough.

I was not surprised to arrive at my parents' house, though that had not been my conscious destination. I rang the bell with a hand protected by the sleeve of my coat, and I took a few steps back so as to maintain the recommended distance. My parents came out, in no hurry, each of them carrying a folding chair under an arm, arranging it in the front yard, a few meters from the sidewalk. There was serenity in their movements, peace almost, as if the meeting were in no way exceptional. Though they are these peaceable beings, they had themselves once been the dissidents, they had themselves been the subversives, the clandestine militants rising up against the dictatorship of other decades; they are now those more vulnerable to illness, and yet they resist, they survive calmly, ignoring my fear.

I don't remember what we talked about, but I have a vivid memory of the picture they formed before my eyes, their pale faces furrowed by the decades, in the background my childhood home, its walls stained by the years of happy neglect, above the roof the top of the tree we planted together, on a distant day that has become present. Time was living in this house, and just being here was enough for me to feel that it would keep running on, in an uncountable chain of events, and that one day time would erase the dark men governing us, and it would erase my parents, and it would erase me too, and it would keep running along the streets, across the squares, the whole city, leaving a whole future in its wake. There might have been something dizzying, something terrible in that thought, and yet, I don't know, at that moment the certainty of time offered me only peace.

PRUDENT GIRLS
BY RIVERS SOLOMON

erusha didn't get where people had been going before lockdown, anyway. Besides the bowling alley—off-limits for Jerry now that the owners had gotten a beer license—there wasn't much in Caddo, Texas, as far as things to do.

On Embarcadero, you had the H-E-B, the Jo-Ann Fabric, the car dealership, and the Hobby Lobby; off the service road, the Chili's, the Rosalita's, and the Best Western. In the strip mall where Lawrence Tate was shot down by the police, bears and balloons marking the spot, there was a Walmart, a Ross Dress for Less, and a Starbucks, and down the way from there stood the gun store and range. As for the library, Jerry never went because the woman who worked the front desk didn't let Black people or Mexicans check out more than two books at once despite the official limit being 10. "You don't want to take on more than you can handle or you'll end up with late fees you can't pay. Start with two, and prove you can return those on time."

Five miles outside the city limits, the Caddo Creek Women's Facility didn't count as part of the town proper, which was a shame, because that was where Jerry's mother was nine years into a 13-year sentence. It was the only place around here worth a damn—and Caddo wouldn't even have that going for it once Jerry broke the woman out.

Nobody watching KBCY newscasters gravely explain quarantine procedures on Channel 4 could really think they were missing out on much.

"Jerusha, baby. Turn that noise off," Aint Rita called from where she sat at the kitchen table. She was doing her daily cryptogram while waiting for Judge Mathis to come on in an hour. "I don't know why these people think any of these measures matter when it is God who decides the fate of man. Let me see Governor Abbott repent on live TV, then maybe I'll make time for what he's got to say. Nothing's going to stop the Armageddon."

But Proverbs 22:3 said that the shrewd man sees danger and conceals himself from it, and it's the foolish one who keeps on ahead, for he will suffer the penalties. Wasn't Aint Rita worried about people dying of the virus? Uncle Charles had COPD, and Aint Wilma had lupus and diabetes. Aint Rita herself was on dialysis.

Most of all, there was Jerry's mama, trapped in a crowded facility without masks or hand sanitizer. It was bad enough without considering she was also living with asthma, hepatitis, and HIV.

Did Aint Rita want her niece to die? Probably. Jerry's mama was an apostate, and to Aint Rita, that was worse than dead.

Jerry was a judicious girl and didn't speak these thoughts

aloud. Like the shrewd man extolled in Scripture, she avoided the danger that was her great-aunt. A girl who knew how to conceal herself from those who would do her harm had more freedom in the world than the girl who flaunted her supposed freedoms to her enemy unthinkingly.

"I said turn it off, 'Rusha."

Jerry pressed mute and turned on the closed captioning. Absorbed in her puzzle, Aint Rita wouldn't notice the TV wasn't actually off.

"You think I'll still be able to visit Mama tomorrow?" Jerusha asked.

The grunt Aint Rita made was either acknowledgment or dismissal. Sipping from her mug of peppermint tea, eyes on her cryptogram, she was in me-time mode, that part of the day when she didn't bother herself with what she called Jerry's antics.

"I could look it up online," Jerusha suggested, playing with fire but intentionally so. If she never said or did things that Aint Rita didn't like, the woman would think she was hiding something. Plus, being able to assert rank over her great-niece gave her a sense of purpose. No reason to take that from her. Very soon, she'd no longer have even that small pleasure.

Aint Rita tapped her ballpoint pen against the table, brow scrunched. "No need to bring the internet into it," she said. "I'll call the ombudsman hotline tomorrow morning and see if visitations are on."

Her Aint Rita would do no such thing, but that didn't

matter because Jerry had no intentions of taking the bus out to see her mother tomorrow. The two of them would be long gone by then.

When Michael Pierce, warden at Caddo Creek Women's Facility, killed his wife with a blow to the head, he couldn't know anyone was watching. His daughters were staying at their grandparents' cabin, and his dog, Sand Dune, was out back. It wasn't a planned act of violence, but he did, as anyone does before committing a forbidden act, calculate the odds of his capture. Because of quarantine, Michael's wife wouldn't be missed for weeks or more, which gave him time to plan an effective cover-up. He had, he thought, accidentally come up with the perfect murder.

Had Warden Pierce been a man of sounder judgment, he might have taken seriously the files for three potential baby-sitters his wife had presented him 14 months ago so that she could begin taking night classes. He'd have checked Jerry's references and found them wanting. Not because she didn't have good references available, but because she didn't want her clients to find out she charged different people different rates based on what she thought she could get from whom. He'd have chosen Jessi Tyler or Isabel Emerson instead. Neither of them kept hidden cameras in their clients' homes after the time they'd been accused of stealing.

But when Michael's wife presented him the information she'd carefully gathered into manila folders, he turned up the volume on the poker match he was watching on

ESPN and said: "Whatever, hun. Maybe ask me after this is over?"

His wife chose the girl who was rumored to be a Jehovah's Witness because she'd heard they were a cult, and she had fantasies of helping the girl escape like she'd seen on TV where people saved young Mormon girls from polygamist marriage.

And it would be good for her daughters to spend some time with a girl who dressed so modestly. None of that hoochie-mama crap. No. Nice, sensible clothes for nice, sensible girls.

Were he a better man, he might have talked to this babysitter who'd been working for him over a year once or twice, and if he had, she might have had softer feelings for him and been more merciful about it all, but he hadn't. He didn't even know her name. Something biblical-sounding, the warden thought. Mostly he knew her as the Black girl.

It was this fact that had started the fight with his wife. Jerusha had come by to pick up her last envelope of cash early ahead of the lockdown. After she left, the warden asked his wife half-jokingly: "Why do they all have butts and tits like strippers? What is she, fifteen? Sixteen? That's not natural." He shook his head as if to say, what has become of the world, and well, what had become of it? Caddo used to be different.

"You're not supposed to say stuff like that, Michael. They can't help it," his wife said. It was always something with her.

"It's just, are you buying that whole good-girl Christian thing?" he asked. He'd seen her looking at him, and yes, he'd looked back, and yes, he'd seen the solicitations implicit in the way her body moved.

"Well, if you wanted me to hire someone else, you should've looked at the files. I'll fire her if you want."

"I didn't say you had to fire her. Don't be dramatic. And what files? What are you even talking about?"

She shook her head. "The files, Michael."

His wife had always been jealous, said he never paid attention to her, but the thing was, if she had interesting things to say, he would have.

Then later she'd accused him of wanting to have sex with the girl, which was ridiculous, ri-dic-u-lous. It was she who'd imposed her body on him, and if he'd taken her, which, yes, he admitted he had, it was not a matter of want but senseless provocation.

His wife had shoved him and called him a pervert, which was, in its own way, verbal abuse.

Blackmail was like the prison system itself. There was just no getting out of it without a little blood. When a stranger sends a video to you anonymously and in that video you're murdering your wife, well, there was nothing to do but meet the stranger's demands.

To a point. Warden Pierce would orchestrate Rochelle Hayes's escape, but he would follow her until the black-mailer was revealed and end it himself.

• • •

Jerry set the table with Kool-Aid, salmon croquettes, instant mashed potatoes, green beans, and crescent rolls. "Well, look at this," Aint Rita said.

"I froze extra, too."

"You been cooking up a storm these last few weeks. The chest freezer out back is gonna burst. The virus got you all scared?" Aint Rita asked.

Jerry got the roll of paper towels and set it at the center of the table. "I'm not scared. Jehovah provides for the faithful. Days of peace are coming," she said.

"Amen to that. Will you do the blessing tonight, or shall I?"

Jerry sat across from her great-aunt for the last meal they'd share together. "I'll do it," she said. Aint Rita's prayers tended to drag. "Jehovah, we thank you for the bounty before us, and we ask that you bless it to the nourishment of our bodies. In Jesus's name we pray, amen."

"Amen."

Jerry had packed two portions of the evening's meal in a cooler to bring with her tonight. It would be her mother's first taste of real food in almost a decade. There were also nuts, fruit, bottled water, crackers, bread, and packs of seasoned tuna set aside. Stores were empty, but the Witness in Jerry meant that she always found herself prepared.

"You're quiet tonight," Aint Rita said.

Jerry spooned a second helping of mashed potatoes onto her plate. "Just thinking."

"About?"

"The end of the world," Jerry said, meaning the end of her life here with Aint Rita. "My mother said when I was born, I heralded in her own personal End of Days, but that that was good. She says I'm the reason she left Jehovah."

Aint Rita's cutlery clanked against her plate. "Shameful."

There was a picture of Jerry's mother with a freshly shaven head taken the day after her daughter was born. She'd told Jerry she'd been overtaken with the urge to cut it all off. Maybe it was hormones, but seeing Jerry born, she realized she could not begin a new life without destroying the old. Rochelle divorced her husband, left Jehovah, and became a lesbian. Shot Jerry's father in the heart when he came for their little girl.

Sometimes killing was what was required, and to leave yourself at the mercy of your old life was imprudent. One had to think these things out. One had to let the new life in, deaths and all.

After dinner, Jerry checked her bags one last time while Aint Rita watched *Jeopardy!* in the living room. She had ten pairs of panties, five bras, five undershirts, three blouses, and three skirts, fourteen socks, toothpaste, a toothbrush, floss picks, mouthwash, deodorant, her Bible, her birth certificate, and a gun.

She rolled her suitcase down Juarez Street, then onto Embarcadero, past the storefront that used to be a Game-Stop but had been boarded up for four years. She passed the Dewey James Memorial Bench, which some Black mamas had fund-raised to install, in honor of the man who was dragged to death by a pickup truck driven by white teen-agers back in the 1980s.

The city was falling apart, yellow and brown weeds erupting from the asphalt. Paint flaking off walls. Before schools closed, the students of Caddo Elementary were moved into trailers because the main building had been infested with mold. The billboard advertising acreage for sale had been peeling since December, only the last two digits of the phone number visible.

There was a beauty to a place as ugly as this, because when one realized it no longer nurtured, it was easy to let go.

Upon discovering her great-niece missing in the morning, Aint Rita would wonder if they had been secretly at odds, but Jerry and her great-aunt had always agreed on one essential truth, that everything around them needed to crumble. A new world was coming if only you were willing to do what it took.

Jerry's mother met her at the water tower, as instructed on the phone. "Did you walk all the way here?" the woman asked.

It was nine miles, but Jerry had worn practical shoes. "He followed you?"

"Just like you said he would. There. See. His lights are off," she whispered, and pointed to a spot 30 feet up the road. There were those who couldn't leave the well-enough that was one dead body alone. He could not have seen her approach in the hazy dark of a gray March.

Jerry walked toward him, her hand on the pistol. There

was no abiding a man who'd done the things he'd done to her. Tonight was not her mother's salvation, but her own.

As was the way of the shrewd man, she hid from her enemy's sights, sidled up, then fired. Jerry had wrought her own Armageddon, and liked it.

ORIGIN STORY
BY MATTHEW BAKER

rom rationing and desperation, greatness can arise! In 19th-century Louisiana, during a wartime shipping blockade. In 20th-century Japan, during a devastating economic depression. Or here, in 21st-century Detroit, during a global pandemic, in a squat pink house. Astonishing to think, for all of the drama that went down during those months in the house, afterward it was all eclipsed by that one event.

"I've had a breakthrough," Beverly announced, appearing in the doorway to the living room in a pink nightgown.

The entire family was there for the lockdown. Her children, her grandchildren, her great-grandchildren, somebody's exchange student from Scandinavia. Beverly's house was the smallest, but she had refused to go anywhere else for the lockdown, and so the family had come to her, bunking on couches and recliners and the spare bed in the guest room. Air mattresses in the basement. Beverly was a 90-year-old widow with a high school education, and though she was grumpy and gossiped constantly and often embellished stories with scandalous details that were obviously invented, the family was devoted to her. Everyone, that is, except for Ellie. Nose-ringed and tattooed, Ellie was a freshman in college, and although the two of them had adored each other when Ellie was younger, as Ellie had gotten older the relationship between the two had soured, and for years she and Beverly had hardly spoken. Perhaps it was precisely because the two had once been so close, inseparable at family gatherings, that the rest of the family found the conflict so troubling. The feud had only intensified during the lockdown, now that the two were forced to coexist every waking moment, to share a kitchen and a washing machine and a bathroom with a finicky toilet. Ellie seemed especially bitter about the ice cream. The space in the fridge was limited, the supermarket had been rocked by shortages, and, in order to make the supplies last, Beverly had instituted a strict rationing system. The daily allotment for ice cream was meager: for each person in the house, only one scoop a night. It was that or run out of ice cream immediately and have no ice cream at all, and so the rest of the family had accepted this as the best solution, albeit a sad one. Every night for a week the family had sat around the living room together, eating single scoops of ice cream with a sense of deprivation. Ellie had been particularly vocal about how frustrated she was by the situation. But now the family saw that Beverly stood in the doorway with a bowl in her hands.

"What the hell is that?" Ellie said.

"An innovation," Beverly said.

In the bowl a scoop of ice cream sprinkled with crushed

254

ice sat atop a heaping mound of crushed ice. Beverly explained that she had made the crushed ice by filling a plastic bag with ice cubes from the fridge and then beating on the ice cubes awhile with a rubber mallet. This, she said, would be a game changer.

"Please tell me you're joking," Ellie said.

"Now each of us can have a full bowl," Beverly said.

"Nobody wants to eat watered-down ice cream," Ellie said, disgusted.

"I would be happy to try," the exchange student said.

"I call it ice ice cream," Beverly said.

"Ice ice cream," the exchange student repeated, with a sense of wonder.

"That is the dumbest possible name you could have given it," Ellie said.

"I actually spent a lot of time deciding what to call it," Beverly said.

"Saying 'ice' twice is redundant," Ellie said.

The exchange student, whose name honestly most of the family could never remember, displayed a masterful grasp of the English language by suggesting that in fact the repetition of ice might serve a valuable purpose, syntactically, in that what English speakers referred to as ice cream didn't literally contain pieces of ice.

"I've never hated anything more in my life," Ellie said.

Beverly made ice ice cream for everyone that night, shuffling back and forth from the kitchen, and although nobody in the family liked having to eat watered-down ice cream, the appeal of having more in the bowl was undeniable. For the rest of the lockdown, the family ate ice ice cream in the living room together every night, carefully getting some ice cream and some crushed ice in each spoonful. Only Ellie refused. She wouldn't even try it. Instead, each night she ate plain ice cream, a single scoop in an otherwise empty bowl. After she finished, she would glare stubbornly at the carpet while the rest of the family continued eating, savoring every bite.

"You know, there's something about this that's kinda nice," Beverly said thoughtfully one night, moments after swallowing a spoonful.

Across the living room, Ellie snorted in contempt.

Beverly died in her sleep a month after the lockdown was lifted, and not until decades later did the family learn about chicory coffee and rice tea. In 19th-century Louisiana, forced to ration supplies during a blockade, people had begun adding chicory root as a filler to coffee, but by the time the war ended the state had developed a taste for the drink, and chicory coffee remained popular there to this day; in 20th-century Japan, forced to ration supplies during a depression, people had begun adding roasted rice as a filler to tea, but by the time the economy recovered the country had developed a taste for the drink, and rice tea remained popular there to this day. Nobody in the family had ever even tasted chicory coffee or rice tea, and yet the family came to feel a powerful sense of connection with those events, because the same phenomenon had occurred with ice ice cream. Even after the pandemic, the family continued to eat ice ice cream—at first occasionally, out of nostalgia, but then routinely, until finally with some astonishment the family actually came to prefer it. The wonderfully gritty texture of the crystals of ice in the ice cream. The gloriously smooth feel of the shards of ice in the ice cream. How the ice would make the melting ice cream glitter beautifully in the light. Eventually the creation was introduced to friends of the family, to co-workers and classmates, and from there even to total strangers. One summer a café in the old neighborhood added ice ice cream to the menu, and by the next summer there were stands serving ice ice cream along the river. A local news program did a story about tourists trying ice ice cream for the first time. In a newspaper article, the mayor referred to ice ice cream as a cultural treasure. The family experienced all of this with a sense of awe. Beverly had lived for 90 years, and to be honest, by that final decade of her life the family had come to think of her as a relic. Even she had spoken that way, as if the great events of her life were behind her. And yet only then, at the very end, shuffling about the house in pink slippers and a matching nightgown with her hearing aid chirping from a low battery, had she done the thing she would be remembered for. She had created a sensation.

Yet the greatest surprise in the whole saga was an incident that occurred before the family ever even left the house. On the day the lockdown was lifted, before she would allow Ellie to leave, Beverly forced her great-granddaughter to sit in a chair in the kitchen and eat a bowl of ice ice cream. Ellie ate each spoonful with a bitter scowl, grimacing with every swallow, commenting between bites on how the ice absolutely ruined the ice cream, how there had never been a greater atrocity in the history of the culinary arts, how the very concept was so utterly abominable that angels were probably weeping in heaven, and how, by the way, she still thought the name was dumb. When she finally set aside the empty bowl, she looked at her great-grandmother, who was staring at her with a neutral expression.

"What?" Ellie said.

Beverly suddenly began to laugh, putting her hand to her forehead with a look of helplessness, and Ellie smiled in bewilderment.

"You can't fool me," Beverly said.

"I'm being serious," Ellie insisted.

Beverly had to lean back against the counter for balance, laughing so hard now that her shoulders were shaking, and seeing her cracking up, Ellie began to laugh, too, at first attempting to keep the laughter from breaking out, her mouth quivering from the strain of keeping a straight face, but then finally bursting out laughing with her face in her hands.

"You only came up with the idea to mess with me," Ellie said.

"I was just trying to help," Beverly insisted.

The two seemed caught in a loop. The harder that Beverly laughed, the harder Ellie would laugh, until eventually there in the kitchen the two were doubled up laughing together, in tears.

"What are we even laughing about?" Beverly said.

Afterward neither of them had been able to explain what was so funny. In that moment, though, something seemed to have been released between them. Ellie even let Beverly hug her, one last time, on the way out the door.

TO THE WALL ☼ BY ESI EDUGYAN

Four years before the outbreak, I traveled into the snowbound hills west of Beijing with my first husband, Tomas.

He was an installation artist from Lima who was working at the time on a replica of a 10th-century cloister. Years before, he became obsessed with the story of a nun in medieval France who awoke screaming one morning and couldn't stop. She was joined over the following days by another sister, then another, until the whole convent echoed with their cries. They only quieted when the local soldiers threatened to beat them. What compelled Tomas, I think, was the lack of choice in these women's lives, in their fates, placed as girls in convents by parents who didn't want them, or couldn't support them. The screaming seemed like a choice that they could make. In any case, he was struggling with the project. At the time of our trip, he didn't think he'd finish it, and neither did I. Already then, something was going out of him.

But that morning of our journey out to see the Great Wall, the hours felt whole and unspoiled. We had been bickering for weeks, but the novelty of the Chinese countryside, with its strange textures and weather and food, had shifted things between us. Tomas grinned as we arrived at the tourists' entrance, his teeth very straight and white in his narrow face.

Vendors along the stone path called to us, their breath clouding on the air. A woman hollered for us to buy polished jade paperweights and shimmering cloth wallets, fake money tied with red string and transparent pens in which small plastic boats floated through viscous liquid as if journeying up the Yangtze. The wind was sharp and fresh, with an almost grasslike scent you didn't get in the city.

We crawled into the glass cable car that would carry us to the upper paths. As it began to lurch its way across the canyon, above trees black as night water, we laughed nervously. Then we were up, finally, walking the ancient stone corridor, the pale light cold on our foreheads. The air tasted faintly of metal.

"Should we have bought something back there, from that woman?" I said. "For my mother?"

"Gabriel wants Chinese cigarettes," Tomas said, his dark eyes watering in the strong wind. "I don't know. Somehow it's more stylish to smoke foreign ones."

"You're hard on him," I said.

I shouldn't have said it. Tomas glanced at me, quiet. He didn't like to talk about his brother much in those days. Between them lay a gentle hatred whose childhood roots were still murky to me, despite a decade of marriage. It could only be made worse, later, by the accident that happened two years after we returned from China. Tomas would strike his nephew with his car, killing the boy. The child just three. By then Tomas and I had entered the era of our disaffection. What I'd know I'd learn through a mutual friend. The death would be a barrier through which nothing could pass, and everyone connected with it would disappear on the far side, lost.

But that day, over the coming hours, the twisting rock path stretched out before us into the distant fog. We walked along a section that had purple veining on the stones, as well as starker, whiter rock, and stone of such muddy gray you felt intensely how ancient and elemental it was. And though we spoke easily, laughing, I could feel—we both could—the shadow of my earlier remark.

The fog grew heavier. Snow began to fall.

It seemed the right time to leave. We retraced our steps back to the glass cable-car entrance, but it was nowhere to be found. We tried another path, but it ended in a lookout. We stared at each other. The snow got thicker.

Behind us, a sudden figure was striding away. Tomas called out to the man, but as we rounded the corner, he was gone.

The afternoon was growing darker. A strong smell of soil filled the air. We ascended a set of crooked steps that led onto a landing that stopped abruptly at a barrier. Another set descended to a solid wall. One path seemed to stretch into nowhere, and we gave up following it. My fingertips began to burn with cold. I pictured Beijing at this hour, the bright restaurants on the street near our hotel, the air smelling of exhaust and fried meat and sun-warmed blossoms, their fallen petals like drops of pale wax on the pavement.

"We are in an Escher drawing," Tomas cried, strangely elated.

I smiled, too, but shivering, the wind a high whistle in my ears. Snow had clotted on my eyelashes, so that I blinked hard.

Two dark-haired women appeared then, a cluster of canisters at their feet. I was surprised to see a mild disappointment in Tomas's face. I began to gesture and explain we were lost. They listened without expression, their wet wrinkles glistening. Then one turned to Tomas, and speaking shyly in Mandarin, she lifted her ancient hands and brushed the flakes of ice from his hair. He gave a boyish laugh, delighted.

The second woman drew from a canister by her feet two foam cups steaming with tea. When she had poured these, or how she'd managed to keep the water hot on so cold a day high up in those hills, I did not know. But Tomas took his with great ceremony. I waved mine away.

The women gestured behind them, and there they were—the cable cars. The glass domes swayed over the open black valley as if newly restored.

Tomas made a noise of astonishment. As we went toward the cable cars, he spoke in wonder at the feel of the woman's palms on his head, their surprising weight, the roughness of her skin.

But on the drive back to Beijing, we said little. It felt strange not to talk, after so long. Tomas was always garrulous in his moments of happiness, but now he seemed emptied, as if something had been slowly forced out of him. As we reached the hotel, I could tell by the tension in his mouth that he was still troubled by a thing I couldn't quite grasp. Gently, I took his hand. He gripped mine back, as if he knew where our lives were going, as if the ravages had already happened. All over the world there were lights going out, even then.

BARCELONA: OPEN CITY BY JOHN WRAY

avi's luck turned on Day 1 of the curfew. He'd been unemployed for a month, he told me—let go from a job selling homeowner's insurance to defenseless little grandmothers over the phone—and he'd pretty much been in free fall since then; but the lockdown changed everything. Overnight, people stopped asking him if he'd found a new job yet, and if not why not, and how exactly he was figuring to pay next month's rent. They blamed the "covirus" more or less automatically, saving Xavi the trouble of explaining that he'd actually been fired for showing up late, cold calling with his mouth full, and trying out goofy voices on the customers to keep himself sane. Suddenly none of that mattered. The whole city was laid off now, and the whole city was half-crazy, and the whole city was desperate to get the hell outside and walk the wrong way up La Rambla and stare mournfully through darkened shop windows at things they didn't actually want to buy. Xavi's life had become everybody's life.

He himself was still allowed to do all of the above, strangely enough, in spite of the lockdown, on account of Contessa and Sheppo. Before the quarantine, he took them out once in the morning and once after dinner—Sheppo especially, a three-year-old Lhasa apso, lost his marbles if he didn't get his daily 15 minutes at the dog run in the Parc de Joan Miró—but lately it was three, four, sometimes six or seven times a day. Xavi took this as a sign that his depression had finally lifted, and that was part of the explanation, no doubt; but there was also a more existential reason. Walking his dogs gave Xavi the feeling of gaming the system, of hacking the matrix, of thumbing his nose at the gods. Eight days into the lockdown, pedestrians without clearance were subject to hassling by the municipal police, not to mention by their own neighbors—but dogs, big or small, mongrel or pedigree, had the run of the town. It didn't take Xavi long to see the business potential in this situation. His miserable employment record notwithstanding, he'd always thought of himself as an entrepreneur.

Xavi put the word out the very next day—first among the residents of his hulking Franco-era apartment complex on Carrer de l'Olivera, then among his friends and acquaintances in the neighborhood—that Sheppo and Contessa were available for "excursions," in two-hour increments, for a discretionary fee. The response was instantaneous. The pitch of his fellow citizens' eagerness disturbed him, in fact. He realized that some kind of vetting process was called for—he wasn't just some sidewalk pimp, after all. He loved his dogs deeply. On the other hand, rent.

He sat down that night with a blue ballpoint pen and a handful of Post-its and drew up an official protocol. Step 1 was an email or text exchange, six messages minimum. Step 2 was an interview of no less than 30 minutes, in person, to be conducted either at the dog run or in Xavi's living room. If Sheppo showed the least sign of ambivalence—Contessa jumped into anybody's lap within seconds, literally anybody's, and was not to be trusted as a judge of character—then the deal was off, with absolutely no exceptions.

To make things even more rigorous, he decided, after long deliberation, that he'd let no one walk his dogs who voted for the Partido Popular in the most recent referendum, or smoked cigarettes, or was nearsighted or epileptic, or walked with a cane. He was providing a valuable service, he reminded himself: decent, law-abiding citizens got to visit their mothers or their girlfriends or their off-track-betting offices, and his dogs got their exercise, and he got out of debt. Overall, as a business model, it struck Xavi as innovative, streamlined, and socially conscious. By the time he'd screened his first client—whom Sheppo rejected in less than five minutes—he was beginning to feel like the Elon Musk of Poble Sec.

The first day's haul of customers was a mixed bag at best: a devout-looking man with a perfectly round bald spot like a Capuchin monk who claimed to need to visit a diabetic aunt in Sarrià; a matronly woman in tennis shoes who told him she needed the dogs for "astral support"; then the same monkish man—who didn't bother to give a reason this time—and lastly Fausto Montoya, a friend from Xavi's old job who made use of his freedom to spy on his ex. Xavi rejected two candidates—one for voting for the Partido Popular (and for being a smoker), the other for referring to the illness that was decimating the global economy and killing Catalans by the hundreds as "Cobi," which just so happened to have been the name of the mascot of the 1992 Barcelona Olympics. Xavi had felt downright righteous as he showed the man out.

Mariona entered Xavi's life on Day 10 of the lockdown, his second active day of business, at the hour when he normally smoked his first joint. She rapped on the apartment door just as he was settling accounts with the Capuchin—who gave every sign of intending to come twice a day, regular as clockwork, for the rest of the pandemic—and stepped past Xavi without a word of explanation, as though they'd known each other for decades. This mystified Xavi, who had been trying for some time now to cut back on his pre-dinner hash intake. He asked her to sit down, partly to buy himself time, partly because she was at least five centimeters taller than he was and he was feeling more than a little overwhelmed already. He brought her tap water in a cracked Real Madrid cup, although he hated Real Madrid with all his heart, and stumbled through his standard interview, feeling less and less like the Elon Musk of anywhere. He began to get the suspicion that he was the one being vetted, not the woman sitting cross-legged on his futon. The slightly dilapidated zone of Xavi's brain reserved for questions of ethics was starting to tingle: For the first time, for no reason he could put his finger on, he entertained the possibility that his fledgling business venture might not actually be something to be proud of. Nothing that Mariona said had raised this issue directly—her basic gestalt simply conspired to make Xavi feel unworthy. It didn't help his moral clarity, either, that said business venture was the one and only reason for her presence in his room.

"Who did you vote for in the last election?"

"What has that got to do with anything?"

"Nothing, really. I'm just, you know, trying to get a more in-depth—"

"The CUP," she said flatly. "My star sign is Taurus. I type fifty words a minute, and I'm allergic to garlic."

Her joke allowed Xavi to laugh through his relief. Of course she voted CUP. How could someone so perfect vote anything else? "Power to the people," he mumbled, lamely raising a fist, which he now saw had a mustard stain across two of its knuckles. "Catalunya for the Catalans—"

"And Covid-19 for no one." She grinned. "Except maybe my landlord."

"That's—a beautiful sentiment. I couldn't agree more." He sucked in a breath. "Just one more question."

"Thank God."

"Would you mind telling me what you'll be using them for?"

She blinked at him. "What?"

Xavi explained, not without a certain self-regard, that he preferred to know—purely for his dogs' sake, of course— what each potential client's motive was in taking them out.

"I don't have a motive," Mariona said.

"But you must have some reason—"

"Of course I have a reason." She looked at him as if he might be slightly slow. "I like dogs."

That shut Xavi up. He gave her the two leashes and the key card to the building and she was gone. It was only after she dropped Sheppo and Contessa off, two hours later exactly, that he realized he'd never asked for her ID.

It was too much to hope for that Mariona would come back the next day, like a better-smelling, less-pious version of the Capuchin; but Xavi was disconsolate regardless. There was nothing to do now but focus on work. Day 3 of business—Day 11 of the lockdown—brought him two teenage girls who claimed to have worked in a veterinarian's office but couldn't figure out how to buckle Contessa's harness; the superintendent of Xavi's building, who was letting his patchy beard grow out like some pudgy, cut-rate Che Guevara; and no fewer than three weed dealers, all of whom paid him in product. The Capuchin came twice, paying his 20-euro fee in a sealed blue envelope that smelled faintly of rosewater, which irritated Xavi intensely for no reason at all. He asked how the diabetic aunt in Sarrià was doing, in what he hoped was a tone of scathing irony. The Capuchin ignored him.

A day went by, two days, four days, a week. Contessa and Sheppo had never gotten so much exercise, and his thoroughly vetted customers appeared to be treating them well. Then—on Day 22 of the lockdown, long after he'd abandoned all hope—Mariona returned. She wore a mask this time, one that looked to have been made from a pair of pajamas; above the paisley-patterned silk, however, her eyes were distinctly more inviting than on her last visit. Xavi knew the desperation born of weeks of anguished boredom when he saw it. He invited himself along on her outing, not even trying to come up with a pretext, and she put up no objection. They strolled slowly up La Rambla to the Plaça de Catalunya, Mariona walking Contessa and Xavi walking Sheppo, and by the time they passed the public urinal by the little boarded-up electronics store at the corner of Pintor Fortuny, Xavi had become aware of a feeling that he hadn't had since the start of the pandemic: the sense that he knew what the future would bring.

She was a graduate student at Pompeu Fabra, working toward a degree in community organizing, which Xavi hadn't known you needed a degree for. She grew up in Pedralbes, a posh part of town, but only because her father worked as a gardener for a rich old man who did something borderline-illegal involving the labeling of wine. Xavi couldn't remember the shape of her mouth, not exactly— she was charmingly strict about wearing her mask—but he had no reason not to think that it was lovely. The high point of their outing, and the true zero hour of their quarantine romance, came when they spotted none other than the Capuchin himself, decidedly not heading in the direction of the poor aunt's apartment in Sarrià, walking an entirely different pair of dogs.

Within the week, Mariona was quarantining at Xavi's place, smoking his weed and essentially running his business. Xavi had no objection—basically she talked, he told me, and he tried to keep up. She was too smart for him, or at least too high-functioning. It was a magical time—in the way you'd expect, but also in a disquieting way, because it all felt so dreamlike, so improbable, that it was difficult to fully believe in. But then again, Xavi reminded himself, everything felt like that these days. Life as he—and everybody else on the planet—had known it had been replaced, seemingly overnight, with some pulp-science-fiction approximation of itself. What was easy to believe in anymore?

Xavi told me this story—his personal lockdown fable, he called it—over virtual mojitos on a Zoom call in May. Barcelona's lockdown had been lifted, and he was back to his old self: unemployed and melancholy, the way he got when he was smoking, slightly too stoned to bring his fable to a satisfying close. Things with Mariona had "run their course," he explained—but he had no complaints. The sex had been great, he'd learned a lot about community organizing, and she'd genuinely appreciated his cooking; but once the restrictions were finally lifted, and everyone was able to circulate freely again, both his business and his relationship drifted off like smoke. He and Mariona had something in common for six surreal weeks; then suddenly they didn't. Things like that happened all the time, especially in times of war or plague or famine. Still, they might have stood a chance, Xavi insisted—they might have made a real home, settled down, maybe even had a couple of kids—if the lockdown had never been lifted.

We were getting to the end of our 40 free minutes, and I tried to use what little time remained to boost poor Xavi's spirits. You never know what might happen, I pointed out to him. Barcelona was an open city again. Who could say what the future might bring?

"I've been thinking about that," Xavi said, cheering up a little. "I was watching the news when you called. There might be a second wave coming this fall. . . ."

ONE THING
BY EDWIDGE DANTICAT

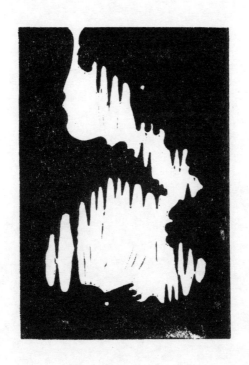

She is dreaming of caves and the rocks and minerals with which he's obsessed. In the dream, he tells her that touching one of the columns rising from the cave floor could cause the stalagmite to die. She laughs and tells him that this might be one reason people no longer live in caves. He corrects her and says: "Maybe not in Brooklyn, but some people elsewhere do. Forced by weather, maybe during or after hurricanes, or during a war. Hiding, or for protection."

He reminds her that there are breathtaking—though he'd no longer use that particular word—enviably beautiful, he might say, million-year-old caves he would love to see, caves with mile-long pits, canyons and shafts, even waterfalls, and with explosions of colors from marble arches, selenite crystals, ice pearls, or glowworms, caves that are so striking they could burn your pupils with their beauty.

He can no longer speak this way, his body vibrating with each word, his fists raised in exhilaration, his head bouncing from side to side, as though he's always trying to generate a room's worth of enthusiasm for the high school

juniors and seniors to whom he teaches earth and environmental science. At home, his sentences had grown short and
clipped even before he became visibly ill. He was beginning to sound like some of her newly arrived cousins, curtly
speaking a borrowed tongue, while the language they've
been hearing since birth slowly slipped away.

This summer, they were planning to visit the grottos
and caves of their parents' birthplace, near the town where
her mother was born, in the south of Haiti.

"One of the caves is your namesake," he said when they
decided to solicit honeymoon funds for the trip on their
wedding registry. The cave had, like her, been named for a
nurse and soldier, Marie-Jeanne Lamartiniére, who dressed
as a man to fight alongside her husband against the French
colonial army during the Haitian Revolution.

"Who would I have to dress as to be able to see you, and
fight for you, with you?" she asks him now. "Would I have
to be a doctor, or a chaplain? Are you—the atheist—even
allowed a chaplain, just in case you wake up and demand
conversion?"

A recollection of his racing breath jolts her awake. What
scares her most now, in this recent hierarchy of terrors, is
not his silence, or the gasping beats of the ventilator, which
is hours old, but when the shift changes and someone
speaks into the phone that had been placed next to his ear.
The exhausted female voice on the other end, a voice she
imagines as a mezzo-soprano in an a cappella group, from
the way her intonation rises and falls so quickly and dra-

matically—that voice purposely perks up and says: "Good morning. Am I speaking to the love of Ray's life?"

How did you know? she wants to ask. Of course they take notes, on iPads or notepads, for one another to read, small details to differentiate, individualize. The night nurse might have been able to make out her words after all. He might have written down exactly what Marie-Jeanne had bawled and blubbered through: "His name is Raymond, but we call him Ray. He is the love of my life."

"What did you two spend the night talking about?" the morning nurse asks. And before reminding her to recharge the phone so she can speak in his ear again, later that morning, and maybe in the afternoon, and perhaps again tonight, Marie-Jeanne sleepily answers in her scratchy, mostly bass voice: "Caves. We were talking caves."

They didn't always talk about caves. During their four-month courtship, between the new science teachers' orientation and their New Year's Eve wedding in the Flatbush Avenue restaurant owned by his parents, they talked more generally of travel. This was one advantage of their profession, after all, their great fortune in having the summers to check off bucket-list items. He liked to describe their planned trips as though they'd already happened. He wanted them to ride a steam train between the river gorges of Zambia's Lower Zambezi National Park and Victoria Falls Bridge, and hoped that before they had children they would climb Machu Picchu, swim with penguins in the Galápagos, gaze at the northern lights from inside a glass igloo. But first they had to go on the delayed honeymoon to her namesake cave.

As soon as she hangs up with the nurse, she imagines driving to the hospital and circling the main building. She'd park under the sweet gum tree by the front gate. In ordinary times, this street would be a conduit to a lobby where visitors sign in before finding their way inside the hospital maze. The day before, she dropped him off on the other side of that building, at the emergency-admission section. Two people in what looked like space suits had wheeled him inside. He could still breathe on his own then and was even able to turn his head and wave in her direction. It was not a goodbye wave. Go on now, he seemed to be saying under the face mask, his nightshade eyes obscured by fogging aviator glasses. There is a long line of people behind you.

She wonders now where in the hospital he might be, what floor, what room. The night nurse won't say, perhaps so she and others don't storm the building and rush to those floors to hold their loved ones' hands. The nurse simply says that they are taking good care of him.

"I know," she says, much in the way he might have. "I know you're doing the best you can."

She thinks that tonight on the phone she will play some of his favorite Nina Simone again. Last night she played "Wild Is the Wind" 16 times—for the 16 weeks they've been married. At their wedding, everyone was expecting some kind of gag, a hip-hop interlude in the middle of their first dance and his abysmal break dancing interrupting the mournful jazz, but they danced the entire seven minutes of the live recording, cheek to cheek. *You kiss me. With your kiss my life begins. You're spring to me. All things to me. Don't you know you're life itself?*

She could call back and ask the nurses to play the song for him right now, but the ward might be too busy during the day. Both words and melody might be muffled by the stream of hurried movements and rush to beeping machines. In any case, the night is when relief might be most needed from both his and her nightmares.

She doesn't realize that she's nodded off until the phone rings and in one swift movement she grabs it from the folds of the yellow duvet on their bed, while wiping the sleep from her eyes. She can hear the Creole news broadcast blasting from the radio that's always on in her parents' apartment as they thank her for the groceries she's had delivered to them. When they ask how her husband is doing, she says, "Same."

When his parents call, she asks if they want her to add them to her call to him later on that night. They could tell him stories, folk tales or family anecdotes, remind him of things he'd loved and treasured when he was a boy.

"Give him a reason to come back to us," his mother says, summarizing what Marie-Jeanne is struggling to say.

"It's not fully up to him, is it?" his father interrupts. He sounds distant, as though speaking from another extension, in another room, rather than on speaker on his wife's cell phone.

"I know he wants to come back to us," her mother-in-law says. "We're praying all the time. I know he will."

There's a funeral that maybe she can help them watch online, the father says, a service for good friends who have "fallen." He says "fallen" in such a literal way that Marie-Jeanne at first thinks his friends have slipped in the tub or on the stairs.

"We were sent a link and a password," her mother-in-law says. She sends the link and password to Marie-Jeanne via text, along with the instructions, and somehow Marie-Jeanne manages to talk them through joining the private funeral group on their laptop. Before she hangs up, Marie-Jeanne hears her mother-in-law ask her husband, "Are you sure you can watch?"

Marie-Jeanne uses the link to connect to the service. The camera seems to be recording from a corner of the funeral home chapel's ceiling. It's a double funeral, a couple, married 45 years, who died three days apart. They'd been at her wedding. They contributed $200 to the honeymoon funds. They are among the oldest friends of her in-laws. The couple's three daughters, their husbands, and four of their oldest grandchildren are sitting on chairs arranged on what looks like every other square of a giant chessboard. The two coffins are draped with identical velvet purple palls. Marie-Jeanne swipes the screen before hearing a word.

Her namesake cave is three miles long and more than a million years old. The first chamber, with the ecru-colored floor, is two stories high, he'd said. Farther in, there are chambers with stalactites shaped like the Virgin Mary and wedding cakes. Inside one of the cave's deepest and darkest chambers, which explorers have named the Abyss, you can hear echoes of your own beating heart.

Tonight she might retell him everything he'd told her about the caves. She would remind him too of how when she seemed hesitant to "plunge in" so soon after they'd met, he asked her to pick one thing about him to focus on at a time, one thing that could make her forget everything else. Today that thing is the caves. Tomorrow it might be Nina Simone. Again. The next day, it might be the bobbing of his head when he was talking about something he loved, or how she could predict his next move by looking past the nerdy glasses and into his eyes.

The phone rings once more, and her arm instinctively reaches for it before she realizes what she's doing. The same nurse who was trying to sound so upbeat a little while ago is now carefully parsing her words.

"I intended to mention this earlier," the nurse says. "There are a few words meant for you on your husband's admission file. I don't know if they were shared with you."

Waiting for some graver pronouncement to follow, Marie-Jeanne answers "no" in such a low voice that she has to repeat the word.

"Would you like me to read them to you?" the nurse asks.

Marie-Jeanne pauses, purposely stretching the time, so if there was some other news, she might delay it for a while.

Whatever the words are, she does not want to hear them in a stranger's voice.

That much she knows. She wants to hear herself reading them, or better yet, she wants to hear him saying them.

"I can email you a screenshot," the nurse says. "Someone's already taken a picture."

"Please," Marie-Jeanne answers.

When the email alert pops up on her cell phone, she knows even before she reads the words what they will be. Ray had written on a plain white piece of paper: "MJ, Wild Is the Wind."

The words look as though they'd been scribbled, in a hurried cursive, with a trembling hand. "MJ" is written in a straight line, but the rest of the words glide down the paper, degenerating, in shape and size, to the point that she's not 100 percent sure that the last word is not "Wing."

She remembers him once telling her that inside the Marie-Jeanne cave, sounds carry weight and travel in waves strong enough to possibly crack some of the most fragile karst. She imagines herself standing at the lowest depths of this cave, in the Abyss, and hearing again what he whispered in her ear during their wedding dance. One thing, MJ. This is our one thing now.

ACKNOWLEDGMENTS

This book began as an issue of *The New York Times Magazine*. Like every issue, especially those produced remotely since the pandemic began, it was only possible because of the hard work and dedication of the entire magazine staff. In particular we wish to recognize Caitlin Roper, Claire Gutierrez, Sheila Glaser, Rachel Willey, Gail Bichler, Kate LaRue, Ben Grandgennett, Blake Wilson, Christopher Cox, Dean Robinson, Nitsuh Abebe, Rob Hoerburger, Mark Jannot, and Lauren McCarthy. Thanks as well to Rivka Galchen, whose pitch for an essay on *The Decameron* was the project's point of origin, and to Sophy Hollington, whose linotype illustrations were its point of completion. We are also indebted to Nan Graham and Kara Watson at Scribner for their support and vision; to Caroline Que, who oversees book development at *The New York Times*; and to Seth Fishman, of the Gernert Company, who represented this book. Most of all, we wish to express our gratitude and admiration for the 36 authors and translators who contributed to this collection with work that has helped us, in ways large and small, understand our place in a changed world.

CONTRIBUTORS

Margaret Atwood is a Canadian novelist, essayist, and poet. Her latest novel is *The Testaments*, and her new collection of poems is *Dearly*.

Mona Awad is a short-story writer and the author of the novels *13 Ways of Looking at a Fat Girl*, *Bunny*, and the forthcoming *All's Well*. Born in Montreal, she currently lives in Boston.

Matthew Baker is the author of the story collection *Why Visit America*, out now from Henry Holt.

Mia Couto is an author and environmental biologist from Mozambique. The second novel of his Sands of the Emperor trilogy, *The Sword and the Spear*, was published this fall.

Edwidge Danticat is the author of many books, including *Breath, Eyes, Memory*; *The Farming of Bones*; *The Dew Breaker*; and, most recently, *Everything Inside: Stories*.

Esi Edugyan is the author of *Washington Black*, *Half-Blood Blues*, and *Dreaming of Elsewhere: Observations on Home*. She lives in Victoria, British Columbia.

CONTRIBUTORS

Julián Fuks is a Brazilian journalist and author. His novel *Resistance* was published in English by Charco Press, and his latest novel, *Occupation*, will be published in English in 2021. He lives in São Paulo.

Rivka Galchen writes essays and fiction, most recently *Rat Rule 79*, a book for young readers. She lives in New York City.

Paolo Giordano is an Italian writer. His book *How Contagion Works* was released by Penguin/Bloomsbury, and his novel *Heaven and Earth* was published by Pamela Dorman/Viking Books.

Sophy Hollington is a British artist and illustrator. She is known for her use of relief prints, created using the process of the linocut and inspired by meteoric folklore as well as alchemical symbolism.

Uzodinma Iweala is a Nigerian-American writer, a medical doctor, and the chief executive of the Africa Center. He is the author of *Beasts of No Nation*, *Our Kind of People*, and *Speak No Evil*. He lives in New York City.

Etgar Keret is an Israeli writer whose latest story collection, *Fly Already*, was published in 2019.

CONTRIBUTORS

Rachel Kushner is the author of the novels *Telex from Cuba*, *The Flamethrowers*, and *The Mars Room*. A book of essays, *The Hard Crowd*, will be published by Scribner next spring.

Laila Lalami is the author of *The Other Americans*. Her new book, *Conditional Citizens*, was published by Pantheon this fall. She lives in Los Angeles.

Victor LaValle is the author of seven works of fiction. His most recent novel is *The Changeling*. He teaches at Columbia University.

Yiyun Li is the author of seven books, including *Where Reasons End* and *Must I Go*.

Dinaw Mengestu is the author of three novels, including most recently *All Our Names*. He is director of the Written Arts Program at Bard College in New York.

David Mitchell is the author of *Cloud Atlas*, *The Bone Clocks*, and *Utopia Avenue*. He lives in Ireland.

Liz Moore is a writer of fiction and creative nonfiction. Her fourth novel, *Long Bright River*, was published by Riverhead Books. She lives in Philadelphia.

CONTRIBUTORS

Dina Nayeri is the author of *The Ungrateful Refugee* and *Refuge*. Her stories have appeared in *The Best American Short Stories* and *The O. Henry Prize Stories*.

Téa Obreht is the author of the novels *The Tiger's Wife* and *Inland*. She lives in Wyoming and serves as the endowed chair of creative writing at Texas State University.

Andrew O'Hagan is a Scottish novelist and editor at large of the *London Review of Books*. His novel *Mayflies* will be published by Faber & Faber in the spring of 2021.

Tommy Orange is the author of the novel *There There*. An enrolled member of the Cheyenne and Arapaho Tribes of Oklahoma, he lives in California and teaches writing at the Institute of American Indian Arts.

Karen Russell is an American novelist and short-story writer, most recently of *Orange World and Other Stories*. She lives in Portland, Oregon.

Kamila Shamsie is the author of the novels *Home Fire* and *Burnt Shadows*. She grew up in Karachi, Pakistan, and now lives in London.

Leïla Slimani is a French diplomat and the author of *The Perfect Nanny* and *Adèle*. She was born in Rabat, Morocco, and now lives in Paris.

CONTRIBUTORS

Rivers Solomon is the author of *An Unkindness of Ghosts*, *The Deep*, and *Sorrowland*, which will be published in 2021.

Colm Tóibín is an Irish writer and the author of nine novels. He is the Irene and Sidney B. Silverman Professor of the Humanities at Columbia University in New York.

John Wray is the author of the novels *Godsend*, *The Lost Time Accidents*, and *Lowboy*, and is a regular contributor to *The New York Times Magazine*. He lives in Mexico City.

Charles Yu is the author of four books, including his latest novel, *Interior Chinatown*. He lives in Irvine, California.

Alejandro Zambra is the author of *My Documents* and *Multiple Choice*, among other books. He lives in Mexico City.